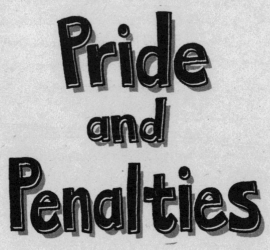

# Pride
## and
# Penalties

*Also by Chris Higgins*

32C That's Me
It's a 50/50 Thing
A Perfect Ten

# Pride and Penalties

## Chris Higgins

Hodder
Children's
Books

A division of Hachette Children's Books

A Catalogue record for this book is available
from the British Library

ISBN 978 0 340 91729 9

Typeset in Bembo by Avon DataSet Ltd,
Bidford on Avon, Warwickshire

Printed and bound in Great Britain by Clays Ltd, St Ives plc

The paper and board used in this paperback by Hodder Children's
Books are natural recyclable products made from wood grown in
sustainable forests. The manufacturing processes conform to the
environmental regulations of the country of origin.

Hachette Children's Books
a division of Hachette Children's Books
338 Euston Road, London NW1 3BH
An Hachette Livre UK company

For Twig, Kate, Pippa, Claire and Lucy. You're ace!

Thanks to Katy, David, Lindsey and Zöe.

In memory of my lovely Mum, Lucy.

'Charlotte! I'm off now. Make sure you and Will come straight home after school.'

Mum, Tracy, a beautician and hairdresser, and the boss in our family. I don't bother replying; she always says the same thing. I've just noticed a spot on my chin and I'm examining it closely in the bathroom mirror. It's small but enticing, and potent, the middle erupting provocatively into a moist white pustule. I know you shouldn't squeeze spots because I've heard Mum say it makes the skin scar but it's irresistible. My nails close up tight, digging in underneath, and suddenly it bursts and lands splat on the mirror, a juicy globule of pus. Disgusting!

The door handle rattles, followed by three loud thumps.

'Charlie! What are you doing in there? Get a move on, I've got work to go to!'

Dad, Bob, and, don't laugh, he's a builder. I dab my chin then wipe the yuck off the mirror with toilet paper and study my face. No more sign of a festering zit, just two angry red indentations where my nails had dug in. I rub them, hoping no one will notice.

'Hurry up, Spider, we'll be late!'

Kid brother, Will, brilliant at everything and adored by everyone.

That's my family, plus me, the girl with three names: Charlotte, which Mum calls me, Charlie, which Dad calls me, and Spider, which everyone else calls me. (Except for teachers who call me 'Pay attention!' or 'I'm not telling you again!' or 'Do you *want* a detention?' Like, yes please!)

Oh no, this is coming out all wrong. I'm sounding like a real weirdo. Goodness knows what impression you've got of me with all this talk of festering zits and a name like Spider. And first impressions count, don't they?

I mean, you'd expect someone called Spider to be long and thin, all arms and legs, wouldn't you? Or am I getting confused with a daddy-long-legs? Anyway, I'm more of a rodent than an arachnid, because I'm small for my age with fine mousy hair that gets in my eyes and drives me mad unless I pull it back in a band, and I'm a fast mover.

No, that's worse; it makes me sound terrible. I don't look like a rat. I haven't got a long nose and sticking-out teeth or anything and I may be small but I certainly don't squeak. I'm tough as old boots, Gran says, unlike Will who's a bit of a wuss. And I'm definitely not covered in zits all the time like Wayne Dobson, the person I loathe most in the world; that spot was a one-off which was why I got so excited about it.

I unlock the door and smile sweetly at Dad who's hopping about on the landing, muttering under his breath about women and the endearing way they monopolise bathrooms. Downstairs Will says, 'What happened to your face?' and hands me my schoolbag and sandwiches and we set off for school. I like walking with Will, he's quiet and it gives me time to get my thoughts in order, so to speak. I think I'll start again. At the beginning.

I was born to play rugby.

You can take that in two ways.

It could mean that I really love the game and I'm good at it.

Which is true.

Or, less probably, it could mean I was conceived specifically to play rugby.

Which is also true.

If you think about it, babies are conceived for all sorts

of reasons, like wanting a girl or a boy to even up the numbers. (Dodgy, you might get the wrong sex.) Or to save a marriage on the rocks. (Even dodgier.) In the olden days, Gran says, they used to go for 'an heir and a spare' in case one of them pegged it. Some kid on telly was conceived as a match for his older brother who had some horrible disease. It was something to do with wanting the stem cells from his umbilical cord.

Wayne Dobson, my arch enemy since primary school, was probably the result of a doner kebab and a cheap bottle of plonk on a Saturday night.

Me, I was conceived to play rugby for England because Dad was supposed to but he got injured and had to give up the game. So he had me instead to make his dream come true.

Dad should have been over the moon when I was born. Trouble was, he got something he hadn't bargained for.

He got a girl.

Mum said he was so certain I was going to be a boy, he hadn't even thought of a name. So Mum got in with her choice quickly, Charlotte Tracy (after her) Ellis. Dad immediately shortened it to Charlie and went down the rugby club to wet the baby's head. When Mum took me out in the pram for the first time, everyone wondered why she'd dressed me in pink, assuming with a name like Charlie, I was a boy. Dad had neglected to mention otherwise.

As you may have guessed, my parents are totally stereotypical. I guess I'm a disappointment to both of them. Dad wanted a big strong son who would grow up to score the winning try in the World Cup Final. And Mum wanted a pretty little daughter to dress up.

They got me instead.

Then Will was born two years after me into the right sex. Dad said it took Mum two goes to get it right. I heard him one night when they had friends round and he'd had a few. I wasn't meant to hear it; Mum nearly died when she turned round and saw me standing there in the doorway.

She made out he was joking but he wasn't, not really. Someone should tell him it's the man who's responsible for the sex of the child. Mind you, he wouldn't believe them if they did.

It's Will's fault I'm known as Spider.

When he was born Dad decided to call him William, after William Webb Ellis who started the game of rugby. But William Ellis wasn't good enough for a rugby fanatic like Dad.

So he changed our name by deed poll to Webb-Ellis.

It's not as mad as it sounds. You see, Mum's maiden name was actually Webb (she reckons that was the only reason he asked her to marry him) so he just double-barrelled it with Ellis.

He wasn't thinking about me at all.

Then came the day in the Juniors that Miss gave us a new book to read together in class. I stared at the cover in delight.

'This is a book about me! Someone's written a book about me, Miss!'

There was my name in big letters on the front cover.

'Charlotte's Web'.

'I thought you'd like that,' she laughed. 'Only it's not about you. It's a book about a spider called Charlotte.'

Everybody laughed and my cheeks burnt. At playtime, the boys tried to stamp on my toes, shouting, 'Kill the spider!' and the girls ran past flicking my hair and shrieking, 'Ugh, watch out for the spider's web!' When Wayne Dobson tried to force-feed me dead flies I'd had enough and punched him in the face. Then, to get everyone off my back, I announced to them I *wanted* to be known as Spider from now on. Everyone took me at my word because even at that age I could throw my weight about (small as I was) and the name stuck.

I should hate my brother for inflicting this name on me

and for being Dad's favourite and for being good at absolutely everything you can think of like schoolwork, art, music, games, you name it, not a bit like me who's hopeless at everything except sport.

But I couldn't hate Will if I tried (and believe me I have) because, even though he's quite big for his age, nearly as big as me, he's as gentle as they come and he hasn't got a mean bone in his body, unlike me who always seems to be having a go at someone or other. And, what's more, he thinks I'm the bee's knees and the best sister in the world and ever since I can remember I've been the most special person in his life.

Like, when he was a baby I used to love running out of nursery school to see him waiting for me with Mum. He was always so pleased to see me, he would screech with excitement and flap his hands and jiggle round in his buggy when he spotted me. Then we'd go home and watch cartoons on telly while Mum made us lunch and I'd put my hands over his eyes at the scary bits (not scary to anyone else but Will could be frightened by weird things like Mrs Goggins on Postman Pat).

He was such a scaredy-cat he wouldn't go to sleep without me so, once he was in a proper bed, Mum put us in together. We'd go up to bed at the same time to a room smothered in posters of rugby heroes going back years, put there by Dad, which suited me just fine. Will

Carling and Martin Johnson stared solemnly down at us as we changed into our pyjamas. Then we'd snuggle under the covers and listen to Dad's stories of the England legends of his day, with whom he would have played if he hadn't smashed his leg up playing for the Tinners, our local team, one Saturday afternoon.

After a while Will's breathing would slow down and deepen and he'd drift off to sleep but I'd listen, enthralled, to Dad's every word, until he switched off the light. Then I'd lie in the dark with Will's soft snuffles for company and dream of playing for England myself one day and making Dad proud of me.

Eventually, as we got older and Will grew brave enough to sleep on his own, I moved back into my old room, the one with the Teletubbies wallpaper, Teletubbies duvet cover, Teletubbies lampshade and Teletubbies rug. I can't ever remember liking Teletubbies. Mum said I could decorate it how I liked.

Poor Mum, she'd have loved a daughter who went for swathes of netting round the bedhead, pink frills and heart-shaped cushions. I was thinking Gothic, painted black from top to toe, mattress on the floor, get the picture? It was Dad who came to the rescue. He suggested England colours.

'How about red roses?' said Mum hopefully. 'A nice wallpaper with the England emblem on it?'

I rolled my eyes at Dad. In the end we compromised and Dad painted the walls white and ordered me an England bedspread. He got one for Will too. Naturally.

Then Mum went out and bought me a new inflatable mattress for when I had a friend to stay the night and Dad said, 'Get one for Will too' but Mum said, 'Just let Charlotte have something for once' and she sounded a bit sharpish.

I thought I'd better not say to Mum that, actually, I didn't have a special friend to invite for a sleepover.

I took Will Carling and Martin Johnson with me to my new/old room but the other day I noticed they were looking a bit tired and yellow and curling round the edges so I went into Will's bedroom to hunt for more posters. He was sitting on the floor, studying a leaflet that had come through the letterbox that morning.

'Don't mind if I take these, do you?' I stood on his bed and peeled the British Lions off the wall before he had time to say no. I needn't have worried, he was too engrossed. I spotted Dad's prize collection of international programmes and decided to push my luck.

'What about these?'

'Help yourself.'

I scooped them up quickly. I could have emptied the entire contents of his room and he wouldn't have noticed. I glanced at him curiously.

'What's that you're reading?'

He looked up at me, eyes shining. 'It's a show, on at the town hall next Saturday. Singing and dancing. It sounds brilliant, like the musical we went to see in London for your birthday. Do you want to come?'

'Nah.' I made for the door, my arms full of programmes and posters. 'Away game. We won't be back till late.'

'Oh yeah, I forgot.' Will's voice was flat. I shook my head. How could he forget? It was going to be the grudge match of the season and I'd been looking forward to it for ages.

Will and I have been going to watch the Tinners with Dad since we were little. It's in our genes, you see. Gran comes to the home games too. She's mad about rugby.

Her grandfather actually played in the Olympics back in the year dot. She's got the silver medal to prove it.

When Dad was picked for Cornwall, Gran says it was the proudest day of her life and she passed the medal on to him. But then he broke his leg and had to give up the game. She was devastated.

So was he. Mum reckons he's never got over it. I asked her once how it happened but she didn't know.

'It was before my time,' she said. 'He won't talk about it.'

But all is not lost. Now they've got Will to pin their hopes on.

When we get to school Will heads for the tennis courts where a gang of boys from my year are passing a ball around. They let Will join in because they know he's good, he's already a legend in the school. He should be too; he's been playing mini rugby on Sundays since he was seven and he's had Dad moulding his career since the day he was born. Now he's heading for the County Development Squad and he's not even twelve.

I stand and watch through the wire fence as a ball is sent his way and he catches it and drop kicks it back. The ball soars high into the air, out of the court. I walk backwards, never taking my eyes off the ball as it falls towards me and I catch it neatly, then my foot comes up to make contact with the leather and I return it in a perfect arc. A cheer goes up.

I'm good too but no one's ever given me a chance.

It's not fair.

I rush out of school at the end of the day, clutching my letter in my hand, oblivious to the comments of Dobbin (Wayne Dobson – he's a donkey, get it?) and his cronies at the school gate. I can't wait to tell Dad my news. I keep going over and over it in my head.

'Mr Brady would like the following boys to remain behind after assembly,' said Mrs Griffiths, the head teacher. She read out a list of names. Year 9 were all sitting cross-legged in the hall on Wednesday afternoon. I'd switched off ages ago, round about the time the notices started. 'Plus Charlotte Webb-Ellis,' she added. My head jerked up in surprise. What had I done?

By the time everyone else had shuffled out, those of us remaining were getting nervous. Mr Brady, the new Head of Boys PE, was not to be messed with. I ran my mind over the events of the past week.

There was the nerdy student we'd reduced to tears in English. Then there was a wet lunchtime when Craig kept winding me up pretending Dobbin wanted to go out with me and in the end I'd got fed up and flicked some yoghurt at him. Unfortunately, Craig had ducked and it had gone all over the notice board. And there was the small matter of graffiti on the door of the girls' toilets saying 'Dobbin 4 Spider' and obviously it wasn't me who wrote it, it was Craig up to his tricks again, but teachers' brains don't work like that and I bet I was going to get the blame. I shifted uncomfortably.

Mr Brady's large frame loomed in front of me.

'Tag Rugby,' he boomed. 'Tournament in a fortnight's time against all schools in the county. I've picked the best members of Year 9 to form a squad. Training Mondays, Wednesdays and Fridays after school this week and next. Here's a letter for your parents.' He went up and down the rows, handing one out to everyone, including me.

'Thanks, Sir.' 'Thank you, Sir.' 'Sir.'

I felt a nudge in my ribs. 'You've got one!' Wayne the Pain leered at me unattractively. Trust him to state the obvious. I was hoping if I kept quiet Mr Brady might not notice he'd given me one by mistake. Too late.

'What did you say, Dobson?'

'I said Spider's got one, Sir.'

'Why does that surprise you?' Mr Brady's voice could freeze the balls off a brass monkey, as Gran would say.

'She's a girl.'

'How very observant of you.' There was a titter and I bent forward to hide behind my hair in case I went red but when I looked up again it was Dobbin's cheeks flaming, not mine, as Mr Brady continued to decimate him. 'Spider, as you call her, has been given one because she's a better rugby player than you'll ever be. I've seen her take the ball off you in the playground. She can run rings round most of you.'

I felt myself grinning from ear to ear. From Mr Brady this was praise indeed!

'The rules say that the best people should represent the school, be they male or female,' continued Mr Brady. 'So watch out, Dobson. I've got my eye on you. I won't have any dirty play in my team. Her place in the team is assured. Yours isn't!'

I almost felt sorry for Dobbin even though Brady's right, he can be a dirty player, then I heard him mutter 'teacher's pet' under his breath and I dropped the sympathy. Me, a teacher's pet? I don't think so. That's one thing we've actually got in common, Dobbin and me, we're both always on the receiving end of teachers' sarcastic observations, especially those of Dale the Fail, our disgusting, obnoxious, sick-making maths teacher.

Because that's the second thing we've got in common – we're both useless at maths (though I have to say, he's thicker than I am).

Anyway, that didn't matter any more, because this was something I *was* good at. To be honest it was my dream come true. I couldn't wait to tell Dad. Perhaps, at last, he'd come and watch me.

You see, I've been playing hockey and netball for the school since I started in Year 7, but Dad had never once been to see me play. It wasn't intentional, he was always tied up with following the Tinners and supporting Will. I can't blame him, I'd rather watch a game of rugby than a game of hockey or netball any day. Mum had come once or twice when she could get time off work but it wasn't the same. I knew she'd only come to please me and anyway, she never followed the game; she spent most of the time nattering away to the other mums and missed my big moments.

But sport was the one thing I was any good at and I really wanted Dad to see how talented I was. I'm not boasting; it's true, my Year 8 report said I was. Maybe now he'd come to see for himself.

'Your dad'll be pleased,' said Mum, giving me a hug. 'Isn't she clever, your sister?' she said to Will who was sitting at the table, munching a big slice of Mum's special rhubarb and ginger cake. I helped myself to a piece, not bothering to sit down. Will nodded, his eyes shining.

'Well done, Spi.'

'Spi!' Mum sniffed in annoyance. 'Why do you have to call her that ridiculous name? She's got a perfectly pretty name she was given when she was born. What's wrong with Charlotte, I'd like to know?'

'Pretty!' I wrinkled my nose in derision. 'I'm not pretty. Spider suits me better.'

'You could be if you spent a bit of time on yourself,' Mum said, tucking a stray strand of my hair behind my ear. 'You've got a neat little figure and lovely eyes and hair. If you wore it down instead of yanking it back into an elastic band all the time, you'd look smashing.'

I brushed her hand away irritably. 'I don't want to look "smashing". I want to look like me. Anyway,' I added, brushing crumbs from my shirt, 'I'm thinking of having it cut short like Will's. It's getting on my nerves. Coming outside, Will?'

'Over my dead body!' yelled Mum. 'And change your school uniform!' I grinned at Will as he followed me out the back. She was so easy to wind up, my mum. Actually, it might be a good idea to have my hair cut short. It would be less trouble and I hate fussing with it. Most of the girls in my class have grown their fringes out and spend all day tossing their heads and sweeping their hair out of their eyes. It does my head in.

Will and I kicked a ball around the garden. His ball skills are brilliant. Mind you, so are mine. Like I said, it's in our genes. We've got a big long stretch of grass, with Mum's plants round the edges and football posts at either end. Pity they're not rugby posts, but Mum drew the line at that, saying she'd have no windows left and the neighbours would complain. I kicked a left-footer and smashed Mum's pot of flowering geraniums. The kitchen door opened. I braced myself for a tongue-lashing.

'Pass the ball, Charlie!'

'Dad!' He came out, white overalls covered in grime, and took up position. I retrieved the ball from the geraniums and flicked it over to him. He dribbled it down to the far end of the garden but before he could take a pot at goal, Will nicked it from him and was up the other end in seconds, placing it neatly between the posts.

'Atta boy!' yelled Dad, raising his arm in the air.

'Dad! Guess what!'

I outlined my news. Dad's face lit up and he put his arm round me and hugged me tight.

'Well done, Charlie. You show those lads what you're made of.'

Dad's big and strong and I fit just right under his

armpit. I grinned up at him, aglow with happiness. He was dead proud of me, you could tell.

'Can you come and watch me, Dad? It's a fortnight Saturday.'

His face fell. 'Sorry, Charlie. I've got a big job on for the next couple of weeks, I've just been telling your mum. I won't be able to make the club games either for a while. I'll be tied up on Saturdays till it's finished.'

'Never mind.' I swallowed my disappointment. It couldn't be helped. Recently Dad has started up his own business and it's a bit precarious at the moment. He's bought a white van with **R Webb-Ellis, Building Services,** on the sides. He says he can't wait for the day when he adds **and Son.**

'I'll come and watch you, Spi,' said Will. Good old Will. I put my other arm round his shoulders. He was nearly the same size as me. When had my little brother grown that big?

'Tea's ready!'

We lurched up the garden together, the three of us, arms wrapped round each other, trying to get through the door at the same time.

'For goodness' sake!' shouted Mum in exasperation. 'When will you all grow up! It's like having three little kids!'

After tea Will had his head in a book and Mum and Dad stayed in the kitchen talking about this job Dad had on, so I switched on the TV to watch *A Question of Sport*. Now that's a job I wouldn't mind having, hosting a sports quiz show every week. Come to think of it, I'd rather be a celebrity on it. When it was over I watched a couple of soaps. Will was still engrossed in his book. It was one of those great big hardbacks that make your arms ache from holding it.

'What's that?'

I'm always amazed at Will's capacity for concentration. He showed me the cover.

*Best British Musicals of the Twentieth Century.*

I wrinkled my nose. 'Bor–ing.'

'No it's not! It's interesting,' Will protested. 'I wish I could see them all. I wish I could *be* in one.'

'Do you?' I stared at him curiously. 'They're all right, but they're not . . . real, are they? I mean, they're just for entertainment.'

'What? Like a rugby match, you mean?'

'No way!' I exploded. 'That's for real. It's a team effort. Everyone busting their guts together to pull off the performance of their lives.'

'That's what I mean,' said Will dreamily. 'It's the same thing.'

'What?' He'd obviously taken leave of his senses.

'How can a bunch of people poncing around on a stage be the same as a game of rugby?'

'Time for bed, you two.' Mum came in from the kitchen, remembering she had two kids when she heard my voice raised. 'Have you done your homework, Charlotte?'

'Haven't got any,' I muttered, suddenly remembering my maths. Damn. Dale the Fail was on my case, with his greasy hair and evil red pen that slashed red diagonal lines and 'Do this again!' across the pages of my maths book. If I didn't get my homework in I'd be for it this time. I'd have to get to school early and borrow someone's book.

'Hmm. Got your things ready for tomorrow, Will?' She rummaged round in his bag. 'What's this?'

She pulled out a letter and read it. Her face lit up. 'Bob! Read this!' She thrust the sheet of paper into Dad's hand. Will still had his nose buried in *Best British Musicals*

Dad whooped and jumped up, punching the air with his hand. 'That's my boy!' he shouted.

'What?' I asked.

'Why didn't you tell us, Will?' asked Mum.

Will looked up. 'I forgot,' he said quietly and looked back down at his book.

'Forgot what? Will someone tell me what's going on?'

'Your brother's only got himself picked for the

inter-district competition,' said Dad, beaming from ear to ear.

'Wow! Lucky git,' I breathed.

'Luck's got nothing to do with it,' said Dad smugly. 'Talent, that's what it is. Raw talent.'

'When is it?' Mum asked. Dad looked at the letter again.

'A week Saturday,' he said. 'Blast, I'm working.'

'It's all right, Dad,' said Will. 'There's no need for you to be there. We're all going on the coach.'

Dad read the letter again and said, 'I'm not missing it for the world. If my lad's playing on the County Ground, then I'm going to be there to watch him. I'll get someone to cover for me.'

I gasped. Will looked at me and his mouth turned down at one side. He knew what I was thinking.

I was playing Tag Rugby at the County Ground. It didn't count though, did it? Not really. I turned to go upstairs to bed.

'Wait for me,' called Will. 'I'm coming too.' I looked back at him, his eyes concerned, watching me, and I shrugged.

I wouldn't have to wait for Will much longer. He'd overtaken me already. In fact, in Dad's eyes he'd overtaken me since the day he was born.

Saturday morning I got togged up in Club colours and went downstairs. The others were all in the kitchen having breakfast.

'Where do you think you're going?' asked Mum.

'Away match,' I said, helping myself to a piece of toast.

'You can't go on your own. Your dad's working.'

'You take us then.'

'I've got a salon-full of perms waiting for me.'

'That's all right. We'll go on the supporters' coach.'

Mum snorted. 'Over my dead body!'

'They can look after themselves, Trace,' said Dad. 'You'll be all right, won't you, kids?'

'Course we will,' I said.

'Dunno,' said Will at the same time.

I glared at him. It was enough for Mum. She went off on one.

'What sort of mother do you think I am?' she said.

'Two kids on a bus full of men boss-eyed with booze – and that's on the way to the match! What happens when they come back worse for wear because they've lost?'

'They're not going to lose!' I yelled. 'It's in the bag.'

'Do as your mother says,' mumbled Dad. 'It might get a bit rough.'

'It's not fair! I've been looking forward to it for ages.'

'Tough! Find something else to do,' snapped Dad, pig-sick himself at missing the match. I shut up quickly. I was used to Mum having a go at me, it was her job, but Dad was the easy-going one.

'Do something different for a change. Go to town with Freya and Chloe,' said Mum, a bit taken aback by Dad's outburst. 'Buy yourself something nice to wear. I'm sick of seeing you in that hoodie.'

I gave her a withering look and stamped upstairs, slamming my bedroom door behind me. I flung myself on my bed. Parents! Half the time they're telling you to grow up and the rest of the time they treat you like a little kid. I heard Dad's van driving off, then Mum's voice calling up the stairs.

'See you tonight, Charlotte. Go to Gran and Grandad's for your lunch. And keep an eye on Will for me, there's a good girl.'

The front door banged shut.

Unpaid babysitter, that's all I am. If I got the proper

rate for the job, it wouldn't be worth Mum working. I picked up *Rugby World* off the floor and glanced through it moodily. There was a tap on my door.

'Get lost!'

The door opened and Will peered around it.

'Can I come in?'

'No! It's your fault. You should've said you'd be all right on the bus.'

'It wouldn't have made any difference.'

He was right, of course. I budged up to make room for him and he lay down on the bed next to me. We stared gloomily at the ceiling, arms behind our heads.

'What shall we do today?'

'There's nothing *to* do,' I said sulking.

'I don't mind if you want to go to town with your friends. I'll stay here.'

'Puh-lease,' I said. 'I'd rather kill myself than prat about in the shopping centre with Freya and Chloe trying on boob tubes and mini-skirts and lip gloss and . . . and . . . glitter eyeshadow . . .'

It wasn't really true; you could have a laugh in town, playing daft games like who can try on the worst pair of shoes and convince the assistant you really want them but they're just too expensive. Freya got caught once – she was drooling over a pair of the most grotesque shoes you have ever seen in your life and lamenting how she couldn't afford them and the next minute the assistant had reduced them to half price and Freya was the proud possessor of a pair of satin leopard-skin sling-backs with diamanté detail. We nearly died laughing.

Another good game is daring each other to go and chat up the nerdiest boy you could find. Or go and stand behind a really fit one and smile over his shoulder so it looks as if you're with him and get your mate to secretly take a photo on her mobile phone without him clocking what's going on. You get points for these games.

But the best of all, the one that reduces us to screaming wrecks, is the simplest. It's when you're sitting in a café and you take it in turns to say you'll go out with the next bloke to walk through the door and all these poor unsuspecting guys come in and wonder why this gang of girls is in stitches at the sight of them. Once Dobbin came in when it was my turn and I went over the top and made sick noises and he went red and walked out again and everyone howled. I felt mean then. Maybe we're getting a bit old to be messing about like that.

Anyway, it was too late to arrange anything with Freya and Chloe – they always needed two days' notice in writing so they could straighten their hair and do a full body wax before they were fit to be seen in public.

And the thing is, though I would never admit this to

them or anyone else, sometimes they made me feel a bit like a spare part hanging round with them. They didn't do it deliberately, they were always nice to me, but they were the bezzies, not me.

It would be nice to have a best mate.

A big sigh filled my chest and brought my shoulders up nearly to my ears before escaping noisily. Will looked at me.

'Might as well go to Gran's,' he suggested. 'I'm hungry anyway.'

I perked up. 'It's shepherd's pie!'

That's one thing you can always rely on from my gran. A good feed, accompanied by an opinionated account of how the Tinners are doing, served up with a spicy rendition of local gossip.

Gran's a brilliant cook. Mum says she can only do seven dishes and it's true, but the thing is, they're all delicious. Monday is fry-up, Tuesday is stew, Wednesday is bangers and mash with onion gravy, Thursday is chicken casserole, Friday is fish, Saturday is shepherd's pie and Sunday is roast, my favourite. Dad says it was the same when he was growing up. At least you always know what you're getting. And she always makes loads.

'How's your dad getting on with his new business?' she asked, setting down piled-up, steaming plates in front of us. Yum.

'All right,' I said indistinctly, my mouth full. 'He's got a big job on at the moment.'

'That's good. I knew he'd make a success of it,' said Gran, putting extra carrots on Will's plate. He pulled a face and passed them on to me. Mum says Gran thinks the sun shines out of Dad's backside and it's a hard job to be married to a man who's been ruined by his mother. Doesn't stop *her* spoiling Will though.

No, that's not fair, it's not Mum who worships the ground Will walks on.

I glance at Will tucking into his dinner and he grins at me cheerfully. I should hate his guts but I couldn't. Ever.

'He'll build up that business for you to take over one day, Will, love,' said Gran. Was she reading my thoughts? Granddad cleared his throat.

'Or Spider.'

He winked at me. I smiled back. I love my granddad. I remember when I told him I wanted to be known as Spider from now on. We were standing in his garden, pruning his roses.

'Very useful creatures, spiders,' was all he said.

Gran continued regardless.

'You're a lucky lad. You've got a great future ahead of you. You'll be a professional rugby player one day. Then, when it's time for you to hang your boots up, you'll have a thriving business to take over from your father.'

Will carried on eating stolidly.

'Leave him alone, woman. He might have ideas of his own.'

I glanced at Granddad curiously. He sounded grumpy. Gran didn't seem to notice.

'He'll captain England one day, you mark my words.'

Granddad got up from the table and took his cap from the peg by the door.

'I'm going to put a bet on,' he said. His voice was cross. I caught Will's eye and raised my eyebrows. He shrugged his shoulders. He'd noticed too.

'His stomach's giving him gyp,' said Gran, collecting plates. She called after him, 'Put your scarf on, there's a chill in the air.' The door slammed.

Afterwards I helped Gran wash the dishes. She told Will to go and sit down while we got square. I didn't mind. If it was Mum I'd be furious, but it's just Gran's way. She's from another generation. And it's not as if Will tries to get out of helping. She just won't let him.

'I'm in the Tag Rugby team, Gran,' I said.

'That's nice, love,' she said. 'Let's have a cup of tea, shall we?'

I gave up. I didn't bother to tell her how important it was, how I was the only girl in the team. There was no point. I poured the boiling water into the teapot. Funny how old people still use teapots and tea leaves and tea-strainers. And cups and saucers and sugar bowls and milk jugs. What a palaver just to make a cup of tea. I love that word. Palaver.

'Take this in to your granddad,' said Gran, piling sugar into a cup.

'He's gone out, Gran,' I said.

'Has he?' She looked momentarily puzzled, then her brow cleared. 'Oh yes, he's gone to the match.'

'He's gone to put a bet on,' I reminded her, but she was carrying the tray into the front room where Will was thumbing through some old photo albums. I followed her in. It was the best room, only used for visitors, and it's a shrine to my dad. Besides the albums that document his life from his very first breath, the walls are covered in framed photos of him in rugby strip from the age of eleven, grinning into the camera. He looked like Will only cheekier. There's a glass cabinet stuffed full of plaques and shields and cups, all inscribed with his name and, right in the front, in pride of place, is the battered silver case that contains the sacred Olympic medal passed on to him from his great-grandfather. The one that Will is destined to inherit one day.

'What you got planned for this afternoon then, son?' Gran asked Will when we were settled down with hot sweet tea and chocolate biscuits. Yum. We don't get much of a sugar fix at home. 'Anything nice?'

Will shook his head, dipping his biscuit into his tea and sucking the gloopy mess it made. He wouldn't get away with that if Mum was here. I tried it myself but part of my biscuit fell off and sunk to the bottom of my cup.

Will giggled. Then suddenly he sat bolt upright and said, 'Spider! Why don't we go and see that show in the town hall? There's a matinee on at two.'

Genius! I jumped up. 'Yes! You coming, Gran? Singing and dancing. It'll be just up your street.'

'Oh all right then,' said Gran. 'I don't mind if I do. Just let me powder my nose and get my purse.'

Result! Will beamed at me in delight. 'Nice one, Spi. Now we get our tickets paid for too.'

What? Suddenly it occurred to me that Will had engineered all this. He'd never wanted to go to the match in the first place. Crafty so and so.

Then I looked at his face, open and shining with anticipation, and told myself off for being paranoid. Will was an innocent. He didn't have a devious bone in his body.

'Come on Gran!' he yelled. 'We'll be late!'

Outside the town hall a queue was forming. I kept my head down and shrank inside my hoodie, hoping I wouldn't bump into anyone I knew, like Wayne Flaming Dobson and crew. That wouldn't do my reputation any good, going to watch a show with my gran and my kid brother on a Saturday afternoon. Nah, on second thoughts, they'd be at the match.

'Perhaps we should have got tickets?' said Gran and Will started to fret, but it was okay, we got in.

And, do you know, it was brilliant. It was a show put on by a group called Stage Fright and it was real foot-stomping, dancing in the aisles stuff. Most of them were from Will's age up to late teenagers and they'd made up their own musical based on political repression in an anonymous South American country. It explained it all in the programme but it didn't need to.

They had this trio of singers who sang a sort of chorus throughout, linking together different scenes that told the story of a girl searching for her parents who had disappeared. Each scene showed part of her journey and had different kids in it who were acting, singing and dancing, or playing instruments.

It wasn't just that, there were stilt-walkers and acrobats and even a fire-eater. At one point an actor walked through the audience and shot dead a speaker on the stage and the whole audience jumped in their seats.

Then there were quieter bits when people read poetry and extracts from newspapers and we hung on to every word because what they were saying mattered. There was a puppet show to simulate a torture scene and the theatre was silent. It was awesome.

The theme song was haunting and melancholy and you found yourself joining in. I could hear Gran humming along beside me, out of tune. I nudged Will to tell him but he was spellbound, his lips opening and closing as he followed the words. It was loads better than the West End musical we'd seen. I've never seen anything like it. I laughed my head off in parts and cried in others and I didn't care at all who saw me.

At the end there was this amazing finale when this girl finally found her parents and all the performers came on stage together, singing and clapping and letting off fireworks. The audience stood up and applauded and sang with them, then we all cheered and whistled and we wouldn't let the company go. They had to keep coming back to take bows and sing another verse of the chorus. When the curtain finally came down I looked at Will. He was flopped in his seat, a dazed look on his face.

'Now *that*,' he said, 'is what I want to do.'

On Monday we started practices for the Tag tournament. It was good fun but hard work. Mr Brady started us off with an hour of circuit training and then when we were 'warmed up' (his words) or 'totally knackered' (our words), he divided us into two teams and gave us our tag belts. The principles are the same as rugby but instead of tackling your opponent you pull off his tag, stuck by Velcro to his belt, and hold it in the air and shout 'Tag!' Pity, I would have loved to have an excuse to bring Dobbin crashing to the ground. As it was I took his tag at least half a dozen times and he only got me once. He wasn't best pleased.

When I got home from school, Gran and Granddad were at the table having their tea with us. Mum was in the kitchen looking flustered and there was no sign of Dad.

'What are they doing here?' I asked Mum, as I washed

my hands at the sink. If they come and have tea with us it's usually on a Wednesday because it's Mum's half day and she's got time to cook something special. As it was she was attempting to divide spaghetti bolognese into six, scooping up long strands of pasta and trying to separate them on to different plates.

'There's not enough!' she muttered. 'You'll have to have fish fingers.'

'Mu-um!' Spag bog was my favourite. 'Why didn't you do enough?'

'Keep your voice down!' she hissed. 'I didn't know they were coming, did I? Gran was at the door when I came home from work and Granddad turned up a bit later. Here, make yourself useful and take these in for me.'

'What do they want?'

'I don't know!'

I put the plates down in front of Gran and Granddad and watched them scoffing my favourite tea. Well, Gran scoffed it, Granddad was looking a bit embarrassed as if he wasn't sure he should be eating it.

'Aren't you having any, Spider, love?' he asked.

'I'm having fish fingers,' I said. Will raised his eyebrows.

'I thought you loved spaghetti.'

'Gone off it,' I said, frowning at him. My brother can be so dense.

'Since when?'

'Since now.' I kicked him under the table.

'Ouch! What did you do that for?' He stared at me, hurt. I glared at him.

'Charlotte, what are you up to?' Mum thrust a plate of fish fingers and chips at me as if it were my fault she'd had to do them specially. They were burnt with black bits at the edges because she'd done them too quickly under the grill.

'I don't know why you pander so much to that girl. You spoil her,' said Gran, scooping spaghetti into her mouth. 'Make her eat what the rest of us eat.'

I gasped at the unfairness of it. Mum looked as if she was going to explode. Then Granddad patted my hand and winked at Mum.

'Take no notice,' he mouthed. I stared at him in surprise then looked at Gran. She continued to eat her tea regardless. Her chin was bright red with tomato sauce and there was a strand of spaghetti on her blouse. I looked away quickly. Mum gave me a small twisted smile and I felt my anger subside.

Dad came in when we'd all finished so he had his tea on a tray in front of the telly with a can of beer and talked about the business with Granddad. Gran said she'd give Mum a hand with the washing up. Then we all watched Corrie together and at the end the theme tune was the signal for the oldies to put their coats on. I watched Gran dithering in front of the coat stand as I sprawled on the sofa next to Dad. Mum came to her rescue.

'Not that one, Alice, that's mine. Here's yours, the red one.' She held out her coat and Gran slipped her arms in, giggling.

'Honest to God, I'd forget my own head if it wasn't screwed on.'

'We had a nice time on Saturday, didn't we, Gran?' I'd forgiven her by now for suggesting Mum spoilt me. Huh, I don't think so! Gran looked a bit blank. 'At the show! The musical in the town hall.'

Gran's face cleared and she smiled. 'Marvellous! I've heard they've got another one on at Christmas. We'll have to go and see it, eh, Will?'

Will's eyes shone and he nodded his head vigorously. Good old Gran. I got up to give her a goodbye kiss and she slipped a bag of chocolate eclairs into my pocket. My favourite. She loves to treat us. She's the one who does all the spoiling.

'For you and Will to share,' she said, hugging me tight. 'See you next Wednesday.' I could still see a faint smudge of tomato sauce on her chin. I hugged her back.

'What were they doing here tonight?' asked Dad as soon as the door closed behind them. Mum shook her head.

'I don't know. They never said.'

'She thought it was Wednesday,' I said, slumping down in front of the telly again. 'She got mixed up with the days.'

Mum stared at me, a small frown between her eyebrows. 'Do you know, she was more trouble than she was worth in that kitchen. She kept putting all the knives and forks in the wrong compartments and she tried to wipe up plates that hadn't been washed.'

Dad shrugged. 'She's getting old, that's all. Comes to us all you know. Wrinkles, creaking joints, spare tyres . . .' He poked Mum in the belly.

'Blooming cheek! You're the one who's going thin on top!'

'No I'm not!' Dad stood up to look in the mirror, bending his head so he could see the top. 'I'm not, am I, Charlie?'

'Grow up!' I muttered. 'Come on, Will, let's get out of this madhouse.'

We went upstairs into Will's bedroom and munched on Gran's sweets. The room still felt like mine, even though I'd moved most of the rugby paraphernalia next door. Above his bed, in the space where I'd nicked the British Lions poster from, he'd put up the programme from Saturday's musical and a poster advertising it too.

'Where did you get that from?'

'I went by the town hall on the way home from school. They were chucking it out so they said I could take it. I didn't pinch it!'

'The town hall's not on your way home. What did you do that for?'

'I wanted to find out more about Stage Fright.' His face looked closed. I poked him in the ribs.

'What you up to, Billy Elliot? You want to join, don't you?'

He nodded. 'They said I could audition for the Christmas production. They need boys.'

'That's brilliant! They're bound to take you on when they hear your voice.' I gave him a hug. He was tense, unyielding. 'What's up?'

'The audition's on Saturday.'

'Oh!' The inter-district competition. 'That's a shame. Never mind, there's always next year.'

'Next year . . .' Will's voice tailed off and he stared into space. Then he said, quietly, so I had to strain to hear him, 'Spi? D'you think Dad would mind if I went to the audition instead?'

I stared at him in amazement. 'Mind! I think he'd have a heart attack! Will, you're not serious? Tell me you're having me on!'

''Course I am.' He grinned at me sheepishly. 'Honest, Spider, you're so easy to wind up.'

'Don't say things like that to me. I nearly had a fit!' I chucked a pillow at him. He turned away and picked up his schoolbag.

'I've got homework to do. Haven't you got any?'

'Who are you? Mum?' I flicked a sweet wrapper at him but he wasn't having any. He opened his French book so I went back downstairs to see what was on telly. Mum was sitting at the kitchen table reading the newspaper.

'Want a cup of tea, Charlotte?'

'Please.' In the lounge Dad was asleep, mouth open, snoring loudly. Mum came in with a tray of tea and biscuits and pulled a face when she saw him.

'Shall I wake him up, Mum?'

She shook her head. 'No, leave him. He's worn out. He's got so much work on, poor thing.' She sipped her tea. 'It looks as if he's not going to make it to Will's competition on Saturday either.'

'What?' I was flabbergasted. 'But he said he wouldn't miss it for the world.'

'I know, he's pig-sick. But he can't get anyone else to work and if the job's not finished by the end of the week, he'll lose his bonus payment.'

'What's the point of being the boss if you can't pick and choose when you want to work?'

'Well, when you're starting out you've got to build up a good reputation,' said Mum, sipping her tea. 'If he doesn't get a job finished on time, or if the work's shoddy, word soon gets around. We've put a lot of money into this business, sweetheart. We can't afford for it to go wrong. We remortgaged our house to set this up, you know.'

'What's that mean?'

'Basically, if the business goes pear-shaped, we don't just stand to lose our livelihood, we lose our home as well.'

'Blimey!' I stared at Mum in consternation. 'You mean we could be out on the streets?'

'No, of course not!' Mum backtracked rapidly, seeing that she'd put the jitters up me. 'If the worst came to the worst we could go and live with Gran and Granddad. But that's not going to happen. Your dad'll make a go of it, don't worry. It just means we're going to have to make some sacrifices round here, that's all.'

'I could leave school and get a job,' I brightened up.

Mum choked on her tea. 'Charlotte, you're thirteen! I'd get arrested if I sent you out to work full-time!'

'I could do a newspaper round. You could write a note and get me off the first couple of lessons in the morning.'

'Nice try, Charlie,' said Dad, waking up and stretching. 'Pity they've closed the tin-mines round here. We could have sent Will down and then your mum and I could retire and go for a round-the-world cruise.' He yawned loudly and rubbed his eyes.

'School's a waste of time anyway,' I grumbled. 'You don't learn anything.'

'You might if you did some homework. Haven't you got any tonight?' asked Mum.

'Only maths.'

'Well, get on with it then. It's getting late.'

'There's no point,' I said in a rare moment of honesty. 'I don't understand it. I've got to find the area of a circle using Pi. Can you help me Dad?'

'Oh, don't ask me,' Dad shuddered. 'Maths was never my strong point. Ask your mother.'

'I don't know anything about it!' said Mum, looking alarmed. 'Ask Will. He's good at maths.'

'He's good at everything,' I said balefully. 'But he's still in Year 7. He won't have done Pi. And anyway, I don't want my baby brother showing me what to do.'

'No, I don't blame you.' Mum stared at me thoughtfully.

'I'm always in trouble with Mr Dale,' I grumbled. 'He thinks I'm lazy but I'm not. I do try but I just don't get it. I hate maths.'

'We don't want her falling behind, Bob. Her report wasn't very good last year.'

Too late I saw which way Mum's mind was going.

'My report *was* good. It said I had natural talent!'

'At sport, yes. But academically you could do with

some help. Maybe we should get you some coaching.'

'No way!' I saw my free time vanishing as I was forced to stay in sweating over Shape, Space and Measure with a nerdy maths teacher on Saturday afternoons while Will went out and scored tries for Cornwall.

Mum chewed her lip, a sure sign she was about to make an important decision. 'I think we should get her a tutor, Bob.'

'Noooo!' I shrieked. 'You can't afford it, you said yourself. We've got to watch our pennies till the business is on its feet.'

'She's right, Tracy,' said Dad. 'These tutors don't come cheap, you know.'

'We can afford to pay for a couple of hours a week to give Charlotte a helping hand,' Mum said. She used that quiet tone of hers which meant there was no arguing with her and played her trump card. 'I didn't hear you quibbling over money when you sent Will to that rugby academy last summer. That paid off, didn't it?'

'Well, I suppose we can run to it for a few weeks or so,' said Dad, caught like a fish on a hook. 'Just till she's caught up, mind.'

Flipping heck. That's what you get for being honest. I wish I'd kept my big mouth shut. Will gets the rugby academy and I get the maths coaching. Someone up there has got it in for me, that's for sure.

Mum was as good as her word. The local paper came out on Tuesday and by Wednesday she'd phoned around and booked me lessons.

'He sounds very nice, Charlotte. He can do Thursday or Friday evenings or, at a push, Saturday. The choice is yours.'

'Not Saturdays!' I exclaimed, horrified. 'Dad! Tell her! She can't stop me watching the Tinners.'

'You might have to kick that into touch for the time being anyway,' said Dad miserably. 'The away games at least. I can't take you, I've got too much on, and your mum won't let you go on the coach without me. Quite rightly too,' he added hastily as Mum started to bristle at him for making out she was the ogre.

'I said you can choose,' she said, turning her back on him. 'It doesn't have to be Saturdays. And *I* don't want to stop you following the Tinners, you know that. I'll take you myself if I ever get a minute.'

'Or my mother could go along with them,' suggested Dad.

'I don't think that's a good idea,' said Mum. 'She doesn't even make the home games any more. Now, let's get these lessons sorted. Thursdays or Fridays?'

I mean, who wants to spend Friday nights doing maths? Who wants to spend Thursday nights doing maths come to that? Nevertheless, Thursday evening saw me stuck at the kitchen table, mobile switched off, a brand-new A4 writing pad in front of me, awaiting the arrival of my geeky new maths tutor, while the others watched the rugby on Sky in the other room.

'I want you to be ready to start straight away,' Mum had said. 'No messing about now, Charlotte. We're paying for his time, you know.'

When the front doorbell rang and Mum rushed to answer it, I expected her to usher him straight into the kitchen and sit him down next to me without the poor guy having time to draw breath. So when she spent ages chatting to him in the hall I thought, what's all this about? She hardly let him get a word in edgeways, though he did manage a few deep monosyllables. Finally, the kitchen door opened.

'Time is money,' I reminded her sweetly.

Mum looked a bit flushed. 'Charlotte, here's your new maths tutor. I believe you two already know each other.'

Not Dale the Fail! I closed my eyes as my stomach took a dive. When I opened them again Mr Brady was standing in front of me, looking a bit sheepish.

'I'll leave you to it,' said Mum and promptly disappeared, closing the door firmly behind her.

I stared at him in surprise. 'It's maths coaching I need, not PE.'

He smiled. 'I know you don't need any help with PE. You could teach me a thing or two. Can I sit down?'

I'd never noticed before but he had crinkly lines round his eyes when he smiled. I love smile lines. I once spent a whole evening lying in front of the fire, propped up on my elbows, with my face in my hands, pretending to read a book but really creasing up my face into lines around my eyes. When Mum noticed what I was doing she told me off and said I'd need Botox by the time I was twenty.

He pulled out a chair and sat down next to me, placing a pile of maths books on the table. I eyed them with dislike. 'I thought you were a PE teacher.'

'I am. But I've also got a maths degree. And a huge new mortgage ever since I moved back down here this summer. That's why I'm coaching. I need the money.'

I nodded. I understood all about paying the mortgage. He looked different out of school, dressed in jeans and a sweatshirt, not so scary. Most of the girls in my class fancied him and it occurred to me that I could be the envy of my mates tomorrow. As if he'd read my mind he said, 'Actually, if you don't mind, I'd appreciate it if you didn't mention I was moonlighting at school. I don't think the Head would approve.'

I nodded again. I knew all about moonlighting too. Wasn't that what Dad used to do before he started his business? We had to keep hush about that too, in case the taxman found out. I winked at him and tapped the side of my nose.

'Your secret's safe with me, Sir. Anyway, you don't look like a maths teacher.'

He grinned. 'I'll take that as a compliment. Do I have to call you Charlotte in your own home?'

'No way!'

'Good. Spider it is then. And you don't have to call me Sir. While I'm here, I'm Phil. Now we'd better get started.'

I felt a bit uncomfortable to begin with. I mean, he's a teacher, isn't he, whether he's in my house or not and it's not as if he's one of those young trendy ones just out of uni who try to be one of us and ask us to call them by their first names. It doesn't work, by the way.

But after a while I relaxed and forgot he was a teacher mainly because, unlike any other maths teacher I'd had in my life, he didn't make me feel stupid. Funny that, because he wasn't a pushover – I'd seen him make mincemeat of Dobbin and idiots like him at school. But if I didn't understand something he didn't get ratty and say it was my fault because I wasn't concentrating. Instead he acted as if it were the logical thing not to get it and explained everything in clear, simple terms so I could follow him. The time flew by.

When Mum came in to see if he wanted a coffee, I'd mastered Pi and was getting to grips with Probability.

'No thanks Mrs Webb-Ellis, I'd better be making a move. I think Spider's had enough for the first time. She's done really well.'

I glowed with praise. 'I get maths now.'

Mum's eyes sparkled. 'What have you done to my daughter, Mr Brady? I can't believe what I'm hearing. By the way, it's Tracy.'

'Phil.' He treated her to a crinkly-eyed smile and I swear Mum went pink. She got all flustered and pulled out some notes from her pocket.

'I must pay you.'

'Thanks,' said Phil, stuffing the money in his back pocket.

'See you next time Spider – if you want? It's up to you . . .'

He made it sound as if he was asking me for a date.

'Don't mind.' I'd enjoyed it but I wasn't going to show enthusiasm for extra maths coaching to Mum.

Mum said, 'I think that's a Yes,' then she showed him out and there was more chatting in the hall, before the front door slammed. She came back into the kitchen, grinning like a Cheshire cat.

'Well, that seems to have been a success,' she said. 'What a nice bloke. They didn't have teachers like that in my day.'

'Who was that?' said Dad, coming in through the back door from work.

'Charlotte's new maths tutor,' said Mum, pulling Dad's dinner out of the oven with a tea-towel. 'Busy day?'

'Non-stop. I don't know if we're going to get this job finished by the weekend.'

'You'd better!' Mum stared at him, then put his dinner on the table in front of him. 'You'll lose the bonus if you don't.'

'You think I don't know that? We're working flat out. I can't take any short cuts, Trace.' Dad got up and helped himself to a beer from the fridge. 'Want one?'

'No. And you shouldn't either, you're getting a beer belly,' said Mum, nipping him at the waist.

'Love handles,' he said, snapping open the can and taking a long drink. 'Got to have something to hold on to, haven't you?'

'Excuse me.' I gathered my stuff together and made a beeline for the door. 'You two are disgusting!'

I managed to get to the game on Saturday because the Tinners were playing at home. Will was going off for his match and Mum and Dad were working so I thought I might have to go on my own or with Gran. (Help!) In the end I persuaded Freya and Chloe to come with me. Big mistake. They'd obviously agreed to come because they thought it would be a good place to go on the pull and when they called for me they were wearing skimpy tops and short skirts. Freya was excited but Chloe was looking as if she was having second thoughts.

'I don't feel very well,' she whinged. 'I've got a bad stomach.'

'Come on, it'll be fun,' said Freya. 'Craig'll be there. You might get off with him.' Chloe brightened up at the thought of seeing Craig who she'd fancied for ages, and we set off. At the ground we paid at the turnstile and took our place on the bank so I could get a good view of the game and Chloe and Freya could eye up the talent. It was dry but grey and soon Chloe was shivering and complaining loudly. I put my hands in my pockets, slumped deeper inside my hoodie and, at last, the game started.

The Tinners played a blinder from the beginning, with everyone hungry for the ball, and in no time at all they were 24–6 up. Freya and Chloe shrieked wildly and hung on to each other every time they made a try or kicked for goal. It was embarrassing.

It had the desired effect though. At half-time they were freezing so I went and bought some coffees for us and when I got back, Craig and his mates had joined them. Chloe was wearing Craig's Tinners scarf and was attached to his armpit. Freya was wrapped inside Nathan's leather jacket with him. (What a poser. Why would you wear a leather jacket to a rugby match?)

Which left Dobbin hanging round like a spare part. He must have thought I was a bit sad too because he suddenly took a hip flask from his back pocket, twisted the top off and thrust it at me.

'Want some of this in your coffee?' he asked. 'It'll warm you up.'

'No thanks,' I said, eyeing the flask doubtfully. Mind you, knowing Dobbin, all talk, no action, it was more likely to contain value Coke than his dad's single malt whisky. He shrugged and took a swig himself, then wandered off. I almost wished after a while I'd said yes. I felt such an idiot standing there on my own with Chloe and Freya hanging off Craig's and Nathan's necks. Even Dobbin would have been someone to talk to. I hate it when your mates dump you for blokes. Freya doesn't even like Nathan, for goodness' sake.

When the whistle blew for the second half, I was so relieved. To Chloe and Freya's surprise the boys went back to their seats in the stand, though Chloe managed to keep Craig's scarf. I had to smile. They've got a lot to learn about Tinners supporters. They don't put their love lives before a good game of rugby.

The game soon picked up again with the Tinners in complete control. At first, Chloe and Freya both followed it, screaming enthusiastically as the home team slaughtered the opposition then, gradually, I became aware that it was only Freya's voice still shrieking. Chloe, quiet now and shrinking behind Craig's scarf, looked blue with cold.

Suddenly Freya gave a yelp and I turned round to see her trying to support Chloe who had slumped to the ground.

'Stop messing about!' I hissed. 'People are looking!'

'She can't help it, Spider!' said Freya, looking scared. 'There's something wrong with her!'

I knelt down by her side and had a look. Chloe was hunched over, her head between her knees. Her face was chalk-white and her eyes were half closed and glazed. She was dribbling from one side of her mouth and her breath was coming in short shallow gasps. I didn't know what to do.

'Let's put her in the recovery position,' came a voice I

recognised and a pair of strong arms shoved me out of the way and carried out his own instruction. 'That's it, you'll be all right in a minute.'

It was Phil Brady.

He knelt down by Chloe and brushed her hair out of her eyes.

'Feeling better?' he asked.

In answer, Chloe struggled to sit up, gave a huge belch and threw up all over him. There was a bellow of laughter and a cheer from the stand where Dobbin was taking in the whole scene. Phil glared at him and he stopped abruptly, suddenly deciding he was fascinated by the game after all. Next to him, Craig flinched and drew back in his seat, wanting no part of the action.

Chloe groaned and sank back down on to the ground while Freya and I stared horrified at Phil's newly decorated fleece.

'Better get her home,' he said, dabbing futilely at his front with a hanky.

'My mum's at work,' moaned Chloe. 'I haven't got a key.'

'She can come home with me,' I said, wondering how on earth I was going to get her there. Craig was staying well out of the way. Coward!

'She's in no fit state to walk,' said Phil, putting his hand under Chloe's arm and hauling her to her feet. 'Come on, I'll give you a lift.'

With Chloe between us, Phil and I helped her to his car, Freya bringing up the rear. Strapped in the front seat, Chloe went straight off to sleep, leaving the rest of us to put up with the pungent smell of vomit. By the time we pulled up outside our house, I was feeling green myself.

As Phil helped Chloe out of the car I got out my key, but the door opened before I could use it.

'What's happened?' said Mum, looking worried.

'Chloe felt ill at the match,' said Phil, handing her over to Mum. 'Something she'd eaten, probably. Lucky I was there to lend a hand.'

'Poor Chloe,' said Mum. 'Looks as if you copped it too, Mr Brady. You'd all better come in and clean up.'

'I'm all right,' said Chloe miserably. 'I'll just ring my mum at work and see if she can come and pick me up.'

'Give us that scarf anyway,' said Mum. 'I'll put it in the wash.' Chloe unwound Craig's scarf from her neck. I was pleased to see traces of the contents of her stomach still clinging to it. She held it at arm's length.

'I'm never going to live this down,' she wailed. Mum stuffed it in the washing machine and started fussing over Phil, insisting she washed his fleece and the T-shirt he had on underneath. Luckily Chloe's mum turned up and whisked her and Freya away before Mum persuaded him to strip off.

She even eyed his trousers, you know, and I thought,

Please, Mum, please don't make him take his trousers off! but instead she said, 'Go and get something of your dad's for Phil to put on.'

Then she followed me out into the hall and whispered, 'Get that new top I bought him for his birthday.'

And I said, 'His best one? He hasn't even worn it yet,' and she said, 'Yes, go on. Do as you're told,' and gave me a push.

When I came back down, having found Dad's birthday sweatshirt still in its wrapping paper at the top of his wardrobe, Mum and Phil were having a coffee and getting on like a house on fire while the washing machine was whirling Phil's fleece around. He'd managed to hang on to his T-shirt. Thank goodness!

I handed him Dad's sweatshirt and he put it on, then the front door opened and Will came in, kit bag over his shoulder. We all wanted to know how he'd got on so we sat round the table and Phil made him go through the whole competition. He'd excelled himself, of course. When Phil's fleece was washed and tumble-dried, he put it back on and left, thanking Mum profusely as he went.

'That's all right,' she said. Mum's got dimples when she smiles. 'You did wonders for our Charlotte's self-esteem in maths the other night.'

'Mum!' She made me sound like a real sad case.

'Well I owe *you* now,' said Phil and Mum flashed him her dimples again.

'I'll remember that.'

Dad didn't come home till really late that night, after Will had gone to bed. He looked done in.

'All finished?' asked Mum hopefully, but he shook his head.

'I'll have to work tomorrow and pay the lads overtime.' Mum opened her mouth to protest but changed her mind. Instead she poured him a beer and fried him up some steak and chips. When she put his plate down in front of him, he caught her hand and pressed it to his lips.

'You're a good'un,' he said and she ruffled his hair and planted a kiss on his head and said, 'So are you. We'll be fine, don't you fret.' But I caught sight of her while Dad was wolfing his dinner down and she had her worry face on.

When he'd finished she told him how Will had got on and he couldn't believe he'd forgotten to ask. 'Shows how blooming knackered I am with all this work,' he grumbled, then he insisted on waking Will up and making him go through it all for him, game by game.

'Six tries, five conversions and three penalty goals in one tournament,' said Dad smugly. 'You've done yourself proud, son.'

He was still going on about it to Mum when I went up to bed. She must have been bored to tears.

Poor Dad. He never knew that earlier that day she'd heard it all before because another bloke had been sitting there wearing his best sweatshirt, listening to the same account of Will's baptism at the County Ground.

For some reason, no one had mentioned it.

'Do I look fat in this?' asked Mum, swivelling round so she could check her backside. She was doing my head in. She'd been trying on clothes in my room, because it's the only one with a long mirror, ever since I came home from school and she was in one of those moods when nothing was right. 'When did I get this enormous?'

'You're not enormous,' I said, bored to tears with the fashion parade. She looked exactly the same in everything anyway. I watched her as she peeled off the strappy floral dress and pulled on a black slinky number. She sucked her tummy in as she zipped herself up, then she stood sideways and inspected herself in the mirror.

'I look six months pregnant!' she wailed. (Mum's always been prone to exaggeration.) 'Nothing fits any more.'

'Go and buy something else then,' I suggested.

'Can't afford to,' she muttered. 'Not since your dad lost

that bonus payment. Anyway, I'm not going up a dress size. I'm going to have to lose weight.'

'By tonight?' I asked sweetly. Mum gave me a filthy look and smoothed her dress down over her tummy.

'It'll have to do. I'll put my wrap on so you won't see my stomach sticking out.'

'Where you going anyway?'

'Jojo's. If your dad gets home in time. I've booked a table for eight o'clock.'

'Can I come?' Will walked in and flung himself down on the bed.

'No chance. It's *my* birthday, not yours.' Mum expertly outlined her lips with liner and filled in with lipstick, pouting at herself in the mirror. I watched, fascinated, despite myself, as she piled on the mascara, making her eyes look huge. She fluffed her hair up, sprayed herself with perfume and finally turned round and smiled at us.

'Will I do?'

'You look gorgeous, Mum,' said Will.

'Thanks. Not bad for pushing forty even if I am piling on the pounds. How can I lose weight, Charlotte?'

'Exercise.'

Mum pulled a face. 'I was afraid you'd say that.'

'You're not overweight, you just need toning up. Join a gym or something.'

'They cost money.'

'Take up a game.'

'I hate games.' It was true. Unlike the rest of the family, Mum never plays a thing.

'Well, go for a run or something, I don't know. You're the one who wants to lose weight.'

'We'll see. Is that your dad?'

It was Gran and Granddad. Much to my disgust, Mum still insists on babysitters if she and Dad go out. We never get a minute's peace either because if we stay upstairs, Gran keeps calling up to see if we want something to eat or drink. She lives in fear that we will have starved to death by the time Mum and Dad get home.

And tonight I particularly wanted to get Will on his own. Because there was something bothering that kid brother of mine and I wanted to get to the bottom of it.

It was something to do with rugby, I was sure of it. He hadn't really mentioned the inter-district tournament since it happened, even though Dad had talked about nothing else. The local paper had carried a picture of Will, face screwed up in concentration, ball tucked under right arm, left arm fending off the opposition, with the caption, 'William Webb-Ellis leads local team to victory'.

Dad was like a peacock, puffed up with pride. He sat at the table cutting out the picture to send to his cousin in New Zealand. 'Let the Kiwi opposition see the talent England's producing, eh, Will? You'll have been spotted, you know. There will have been scouts there from the RFU.'

Will shrugged. 'There were plenty of good players, Dad.'

'You're too modest, son. They'll recognise real flair when they see it.'

Mum rolled her eyes. 'Give it a rest, Bob. He's only eleven.'

Dad was right though. The next day a large white envelope popped through the letterbox addressed to Mr William Webb-Ellis. It had a Cornwall Rugby Union stamp on the front. We were all dying to find out what was in it but, believe it or not, my little brother was late home from school that day. Even Dad was home before him and when he saw the postmark he wanted to open it but Mum said emphatically, 'NO, it's for Will, not you!' I nearly died waiting but at last Will burst through the door, all hot and sweaty and out of breath as if he'd been running, and no one asked him where he'd been, we all just wanted to know what was in that letter.

He looked at us all standing there and said, 'What?' and I thrust the envelope into his hands. He went as still as a statue.

'Go on then, open it, Will,' said Mum. He looked up at her, his eyes curiously blank.

'You open it, Dad.'

'No, it's yours, son,' he said with a supreme effort of will.

'Oh, give it to me!' I said and tore it open. Inside there was a letter congratulating Will on his performance on Saturday and inviting him to take part in some training sessions on Friday nights with other selected top kids from all over the county with a view to an exhibition match against Devon to be arranged at the County Ground in the New Year. Yes!

I shrieked, Mum shrieked and, you can imagine, Dad was over the moon.

'You're representing Cornwall, son,' he yelled, 'at the age of eleven!' He danced Mum around the kitchen and she called him a 'Big Lummox' but she laughed when she said it which was good, because she'd been a bit off with him since he didn't get his bonus payment. And all that time Will just kept on standing there, reading and re-reading the letter as if he couldn't take it in. Then Dad rang Gran to tell her the news and she and Granddad came round and Gran cried.

And she said, 'You know what this means, Bob. When Will gets to play for the County, you'll have to pass on the Olympic medal to him. It's a tradition now!'

'Blimey,' said Dad, in the middle of pouring a celebratory pint for Granddad. 'I hadn't thought of that. I wasn't expecting to have to do that for a year or two.' But he looked dead pleased.

We were all proud of Will.

The only one who didn't seem overjoyed by his success was Will himself.

He'd been quiet ever since, as if he'd got something on his mind. It might be just the fuss people were making. He'd been clapped by the whole school in assembly and Dad was going round telling anyone who'd listen about his talented son. Will hates being in the limelight. Anyway, tonight I wanted to find out what was bothering him.

Mum and Dad finally left in a taxi after having a piece of birthday cake that Gran had made. She'd put '*Happy birthday Tracy, 21 Today*' on it in pink icing. Mum laughed when she saw it and said, 'Thanks Alice, you shouldn't have gone to such trouble.' And Gran said, 'Well, it's not every day you're twenty-one, is it?' and Mum laughed again and said, 'No, you're right there.'

But you know what? I had this funny feeling that Gran wasn't kidding and I think Granddad did too because he looked at me and raised his eyebrows.

I sat and watched Corrie with Gran while Granddad read the paper and then Gran said, 'What's Will up to?'

and that was my chance. I said, 'I'll go up and see if he's all right, Gran.'

I could hear music coming from his bedroom and I knocked on the door gently. After all, I didn't want to catch him doing whatever it is Year 7 boys do in the privacy of their own bedrooms. (Doesn't bear thinking about, gross.)

'Will?'

'Yeah?'

'Can I come in?'

'Yeah.'

He was lying on his bed, arms behind his head, staring at the ceiling.

'What you up to?'

'Nothing.'

'You all right?'

'Yeah. Why shouldn't I be?'

'You've been kind of quiet lately.'

Will cleared his throat. I waited.

'Spider?'

'What?'

'Will? Spider! Do you want a sandwich?'

'No thanks, Gran!' we yelled in unison.

'You know I'm doing that exhibition match . . .'

'Yeah.'

'You know I've got to go training every Friday . . .'

'Tea or coffee?' came Gran's voice.

'No thanks, Gran! Yeah, so what?'

'Well, if I don't go, do you think I'll get kicked out of the team?' he asked in a small voice.

''Course you would.' I stared at him in surprise.

'How about a piece of cake?'

'NO, GRAN! NOTHING! Will? Why don't you want to go training?'

'I didn't say I didn't *want* to go,' said Will crossly.

'What did you say then?'

'Nothing,' he said, turning away from me. 'Get out of my room.'

'Are you two arguing up there? Spider? Come on down and leave the lad alone!'

I don't know why I bother, I really don't. That's all the thanks I get for being a caring sister. I went downstairs and drank a cup of tea I didn't want because Gran had made one for Granddad even though he'd said no when she asked him.

'I'll be up all night if I have any more tea,' he grumbled. 'Why don't you listen?'

'I'll drink it, Gramps.' Poor Gran, she only means to please. I sat next to her on the couch and she put her arm round me and stroked my hair gently. I snuggled into her armpit. She's lovely, my gran, even if she does go on a bit sometimes.

There was a funny smell. Sort of like stale wee. Bit like the whiff you get from the boys' changing room when the door opens. I wrinkled my nose and sat up. It receded. I moved away from her to the other end of the couch.

'All right?' she asked in surprise.

I nodded. 'I just want to read under the lamp, Gran,' I lied, not wanting to hurt her feelings, and picked up a magazine.

'Is Will coming down?'

'No, he's gone to bed, I think.'

Gran nodded. 'He needs his sleep. He's growing like a tree. He'll make a good prop forward, won't he, Joe? I said, he'll make . . .'

'A good prop forward . . . I heard you. Aye, he will, if you've got anything to do with it.'

I glanced up. It was that tone again. I don't like it when he's irritable with her, he never used to be. First Will, now Granddad? What's wrong with the men in my family? I yawned and stretched.

'I'm going up to bed. I've got the Tag tournament tomorrow at the County Ground.'

'Tag? What's that?'

'I told you, Gran, remember? Tag Rugby? D'you want to come and watch?'

'We'll be there,' said Granddad. 'We're bringing Will in the car, aren't we, Alice? Can't wait.'

'Wild horses wouldn't keep us away!' Gran's eyes were shining, even though she'd obviously forgotten all about it till she was reminded. 'Now you go on up and get a good night's sleep.'

I leant over to give her a kiss and caught a whiff again. Someone should tell her. (Not me!) I must have a word with Mum.

Will's door was shut when I went up so I cleaned my teeth and got into bed and was soon fast asleep. Later on though, I woke up to voices. At first I thought it was the telly, because it was coming from downstairs, then I realised it was Mum and Dad, home from their night out.

They were having a go at each other, their voices rising and falling, each taking turns to hush the other up when they got too animated. They both sounded as if they'd had a bit too much to drink. I opened my door and went and sat at the top of the stairs. Their voices came clearly from the kitchen.

'Do something about it then,' Dad was saying. 'If you've got it in your head you're overweight, then go on a diet.'

'There you are, you've admitted it at last,' said Mum, sounding as if she was going to cry. 'You think I'm fat.'

'I don't, you silly cow! *You* think you're fat! You've gone on about it all evening and ruined an expensive night out!'

'Don't call me a cow! And it is my birthday! I'm entitled to a night out on my birthday. Don't be such a tight-arse!'

'I'm not a tight-arse! I'm working my fingers to the bone . . .'

'So why didn't you get the job finished on time then? Tell me that?'

There was a noise behind me. I turned to see Will standing in his doorway, rubbing his eyes. 'What's wrong with them?'

'Nothing, they're just pissed. Anyway, they've stopped now. Back to bed, you.'

He did as he was told and within minutes I could hear light snores coming from his open door. I got back into bed and pulled the covers up over my head as the voices started up again, Mum's high and agitated, Dad's deeper and more appeasing as if he was trying to make up. After a while I heard them coming upstairs then the sound of the toilet flushing and taps flowing and then silence.

Soon the whole house was fast asleep but I lay awake for ages, my mind refusing to switch off.

Smelly Gran, Grumpy Gramps, Weird Will. Tag tournament tomorrow. Mum's too fat, Dad's cocking up the business. Mum and Dad yelling at each other. Out on the streets, divorce. DIVORCE!

Flipping heck! I thought Will was supposed to be the worrier!

I tossed and turned all night long, stomach twisted into a knot of tension. My bed was too messy, too hot and too high and I felt as if I was going to fall off the edge. In the end I got out and blew up my new inflatable mattress and lay down on that instead, and finally, as the grey dawn light stole in through the curtain, I dropped off to sleep.

I got bawled at in the morning by Mum for sleeping in.

'Whose fault is that!' I shouted back. 'You were the one who was yelling your head off last night when I was trying to sleep!' At least she had the grace to look ashamed. I was so knackered, but by the time I'd eaten my cornflakes, I started to feel human again. All last night's worries receded and I couldn't wait to get on that pitch.

Mr Brady sat next to me on the coach and we got talking. It's funny how I think of him as Mr Brady in school and Phil at home.

'Why don't they have mixed teams for proper rugby, Sir? I'm as good as the boys, you said so yourself.'

He grinned. 'Better, I said. No, you don't want to play with the lads. You want to play women's rugby, then you'll see how rugby can be played intelligently.'

'Is there a women's rugby team?'

He shook his head. 'Not down here, as far as I know. There are plenty up country, though.'

'It's not fair.' I folded my arms and gazed out moodily at the rolling countryside. 'It's not the same anyway, is it, Sir?'

'What do you mean?'

'It's not as good.'

'Who says?'

'My dad.'

He was silent for a bit then he said, 'Your dad's Robert Ellis, isn't he? Played second row for the Tinners in the eighties?'

'That's him.' I loved it when people knew my dad. 'He played for Cornwall too, then he broke his leg and had to retire. He could have played for England, you know. Did you ever see him play, Sir?'

He nodded. 'I played against him myself a number of times.' There was a pause. Then he said, 'You're a better player than he ever was, Spider.' A commotion broke out at the back of the bus and he swung himself out of his seat to sort it, leaving me bemused. I mean, what was he on? My dad was the best. Still, it was nice to know he thought so highly of me.

When we got to the County Ground it was already awash with kids togged up in various team colours, practising their moves. The pitch was divided into two, marked out crosswise. There were quite a few supporters there already, but no sign of Will or Gran and Gramps yet.

We went down the tunnel into a whitewashed corridor where pictures of past heroes hung on the wall. It was quite something and I wondered why Will hadn't mentioned it when he played last weekend. I stopped to have a look at them and one caught my eye, a picture of a young man in Cornwall colours wearing a tasselled cap.

'Look, Sir! There's a picture of my dad!'

Everyone crowded round to see.

'Duh! Your dad's getting on a bit then, isn't he?' said Craig cuttingly, pointing to the inscription underneath.

**Harry Roberts: Olympic Silver Medallist 1908.**

I felt stupid, cut to the quick.

Then the penny dropped. Gran was a Roberts before she got married. 'No it's not, it's my granddad. I mean my great-granddad. No, my great-great-granddad!'

'Make your mind up,' jeered Craig and he moved on down the corridor with the others. I could tell they didn't believe me.

Somebody did though. Behind me Dobbin had stayed for a second look.

'Wow, an Olympic medallist,' he breathed. I could feel myself tingling with pride.

'He looks like my dad, Sir.'

'So he does.' Mr Brady peered at the inscription and tapped it. 'This is history, you know. Maybe one day, one of you will be up here.'

Dobbin and I looked at each other. His face had lost its usual scowl and looked as if it was lit up from the inside. I knew what he was feeling. For a moment anything seemed possible.

'Better get changed up,' said Mr Brady looking at his watch. 'Boys at the end on the left, girls on the right. See you outside in five minutes.'

Dobbin and I walked down the corridor together. As we passed an open door showing a communal bath, Dobbin nudged me.

'See you in there afterwards, Spider.'

'Pervert!' I said automatically but then he winked at me and I found myself grinning back at him. Well, maybe he wasn't so bad after all. I mean, at least he'd been impressed by my famous predecessor.

I pushed the door of the girls' changing room open and walked in. Clothes hung on hooks with bags beneath them, but there was only one other occupant, standing in front of the mirror. Blonde hair, sky-blue tracksuit and, wait for it, putting on mascara. She turned round and grinned at me.

'Hi. Want some? Special non-run, non-smear, for when you get hot and sweaty.'

'No thanks.' I chucked my bag on the bench. Why would I worry about eye sparkle when we had a tournament to win? Funny thing was, I was sure I'd seen this girl somewhere before.

'Suit yourself.' She bent over and brushed her hair thoroughly, head down. Then she stood up, swinging her hair over her head in a blonde arc and parted it deftly down the centre, brushing each side up into two high bunches and securing them with elastic. Finally, she wrapped a length of hair round each band and pinned them carefully and then spritzed them with gloss.

'There,' she said, taking out a can of deodorant and spraying generously inside her rugby shirt. 'I'm done.' She took out a magazine and sat on the bench, flicking through it.

I turned my back to her and stripped down to my bra and pants. I knew she was watching me.

'Want to borrow my body spray?' she asked.

I was about to say no when I suddenly remembered Gran and her BO and said instead, 'Thanks. I've forgotten mine.' She held it out and I sprayed myself copiously.

'I'm Becky.'

'Spider.'

'What?'

'Spider.'

'What sort of name is that?'

I found myself explaining how I got the name and Becky chuckled.

'Good for you. And this Dobbin's playing today, is he? I'll have to look out for him.'

There was no need. Dobbin spotted Becky as soon as she set foot outside the changing room. He whistled and nudged the guy next to him.

'Wouldn't mind tackling her.'

Becky eyed him coolly up and down. 'You'd have to catch me first.'

'No problem,' leered Dobbin. 'If we've got to have girls playing rugby, at least we've got a good-looking one at last.'

Thanks, Dobbin. My opinion of him plummeted again to its original depths.

'Pity I can't say the same for the boys,' said Becky, taking me by the arm. 'Come on, Spider, let's go and warm up.'

Soon the whistle blew for the start of the tournament. We played seven-a-side, ten minutes a game, with no half-time. For simplicity's sake, a try was worth one point. I looked round for Gran and Gramps before we started but there was still no sign of them. I was disappointed but once the game began I settled down and got on with what I was there for.

Mr Brady had put me as captain but I hardly got my

hands on the ball for a while, because the boys kept it to themselves. When he saw what was going on Brady sorted it and once I had possession I was fine, because I'm fast so within minutes I'd scored my first try. By the end of the game I'd scored another two and we'd won 6–4.

The second round was even easier, with me playing a blinder and us beating the opposition 10–1. Suddenly we were into the semi-final and raring to go. We ran back out on to the pitch and I looked up at the stand. Where were Gran and Gramps? Where was Will? Hundreds of supporters all waving and cheering, but no one there for me. They'd promised.

Then we were off and there was no time to worry about my missing fan club. Guess who we were up against? Becky's team. They were good. Like me she was the only girl in her team but she had respect and the boys made use of her skills. I upped my game, flying down the pitch after her to grab her tag.

Trouble was, Dobbin was targeting Becky too and when he discovered she could outrun him, he started bending the rules. First he was warned for running in front of her, then he got pulled up for forcing her into touch. Stupid idiot. The more she outstripped him, the more dangerous he became. We were so well matched it was anyone's game but in the end his dirty play cost us our place in the final. In the last minute of the game with the scores level he tackled her from the front and the ref awarded a penalty to them. They scored, of course. Well done, Dobbin.

We came off the pitch really fed up. I mean, it's bad enough losing, but to give it away like that. I glanced up and saw Will leading Gran and Granddad to seats in the stand. Bit late or what? They needn't have bothered, they'd missed all the action. They sat down looking flustered as if they'd been rushing, and Will pointed to me and waved, but I was so mad with Dobbin and with them for being late that I didn't wave back.

We watched the final from the sideline. It was a big anticlimax; there was no contest. Becky's team slaughtered them, like we would have, and emerged jubilant victors, 14–3. Becky got a big cheer from the crowd when she went up to collect the trophy. That should've been me.

'You're a useful player,' said Becky, emerging from the shower back in the changing room. She seemed none the worse for her collision with Dobbin, though she was sporting an impressive-looking bruise on her shin.

'Thanks. You're pretty good yourself,' I conceded.

She shrugged. 'I enjoy it,' she said, towelling her hair vigorously. 'It's a really good workout. Sod it,' she said, inspecting her leg. 'I wanted to wear my new mini-skirt out tonight. I've got a date.'

I eyed her curiously. She was such a funny mixture, one of the boys but girly at the same time. Just for a moment I wondered with a pang what it would feel like to be going on a date that night. Nah. I finished changing and ran a comb through my hair. I'd rather watch *Match of the Day* with Dad.

Outside the tunnel Will was waiting with Gran and Gramps, looking a bit ill at ease. So he should be. Gran threw her arms around me and said, 'Well done, Spider. You played brilliantly.'

'You never even saw me,' I said sulkily, shaking her off. 'Where were you?'

'Okay, who's coming back on the bus with me?' Mr Brady moved between us, consulting his list. 'Spider?'

'I can go with my granddad if it's all right with you, Sir.'

'Yeah, sure. Played a blinder today, didn't she?' Mr Brady smiled at Gramps then turned to Dobbin. 'Get on the bus, Wayne. I want a word with you.'

Dobbin scowled. He knew he was in for it; it was obvious from Brady's tone.

As we got in the car, Becky came running over.

'Spider! Give me your number! I'll text you.'

'Okay!' I felt absurdly pleased. She passed me her

phone to enter it and said, 'Oh hi, Will. I didn't see you there. How you doing?'

I glanced up in surprise.

'How do you two know each other?'

'Stage Fright.'

Of course. That's where I'd seen Becky before. The girl in the show. Was there no end to Becky's talents? But why did she remember Will?

'Cool brother, Spider. All the more reason for us girls to keep in touch. See you both!'

I waved till we turned the corner, then sat back and looked at Will. He was staring out of the window, avoiding my eyes.

'I still don't get how she knows you.'

'Sshh,' he said, looking anxiously at the front seat. 'Gran'll hear you.'

'So? What are you up to?'

He frowned. 'I'll tell you later.'

We sat in silence for a bit, then he said, 'I'm sorry we missed you.'

I sniffed. It was my turn to stare out of the window ignoring him, then, in the end, curiosity got the better of me.

'Why were you late?' I asked.

He grimaced then whispered, 'Gran forgot about the match and went shopping.'

'No!'

He nodded, eyes wide. 'We had to wait till she got back. Gramps was livid. He yelled at her and she got all in a tizz. How could she forget the tournament?'

I shrugged. It wasn't a bit like Gran. She was always so dependable. Though, come to think of it, she had been a bit strange lately.

But there's one thing for sure. She wouldn't have forgotten it if it were Will playing.

I've done it. I've cut my hair off.

I look like a boy now. I look like Will.

It's Dad's fault.

When we got home on Saturday, Will went up to his bedroom and I sat down at the kitchen table with Mum and went through the tournament over a cup of tea. Mum listened to it all, tutting when I told her how Dobbin lost us a place in the semi-final.

After a while she said, 'Anyway, stop going on about him. It sounds as if you played well, that's the main thing . . . I bet Gran was pleased.'

'She didn't even see me play.'

'What? Why not?'

'Ask Will.'

'WILL! Get down here!'

When Will told her that Gran had gone shopping and they had to wait till she got back, Mum's lips tightened into a straight line. She didn't say anything but she went out to the hall and picked up the phone. Will and I looked at each other.

'Don't tell her off, Mum, she forgot,' said Will.

'Forgot,' she said scornfully, but she put the receiver down. Will and I watched her anxiously. Her face softened.

'How about a takeaway tonight?'

'Yes!' we yelled and I got up and threw my arms around Mum, squeezing her tight. 'Can we afford it?'

'Course we can, love,' she said, smoothing my hair back. 'It's a special occasion, isn't it? It's not every day my daughter gets to the semi-final of a Tag Rugby tournament.'

We kept the food warm in the oven till Dad came home. He looked tired when he came in but brightened up when he saw the table laid with the best plates and a bottle of sparkling wine. Mum put the dishes out on the table while he opened the wine.

'What are we celebrating?' he said, shaking the bottle. 'Got a glass ready, Will? Don't want to waste any of this lovely bubbly.'

'Charlotte's success in the tag tournament.'

'Sorry, Charlie, I forgot. Did you win?' He paused and looked at me expectantly, bottle between his knees, ready to pull out the cork.

'Got beaten in the semi.'

The cork came out with a dull squelching sound, more like a damp squib, than an explosion. A little wine trickled into the glass Will was holding. Dad filled it up and tried it.

'Hmm. Bit flat, I'm afraid.' He took another swig. 'So you didn't even make it to the final? Lucky I didn't take time off to go and see it.' He poured another glass. 'Here you are, Trace.'

'No thanks.' Mum turned away, her face livid. 'Come and eat this, kids, before it gets cold.'

Dad insisted on pouring Will and me a glass, though we'd rather have had Coke. It tasted horrible, sweet, warm and flat, so I left it. We left a lot of the food too; we'd probably ordered too much in the first place. Only Dad seemed hungry, eating his own and tucking in as well to my spicy prawn and Will's beef with cashew nuts, then polishing off Mum's special fried rice. No one touched the sweet and sour.

Afterwards, Will and I chucked what was left in the bin and then we sat down to watch telly. Dad finished off the wine because no one else wanted any, then he poured himself a beer in a pint glass.

'Haven't you had enough?' said Mum sharply.

'Thought we were supposed to be celebrating,' he said, taking a big gulp and smacking his lips. 'Though no one seems to be having much fun.'

'Whose fault is that then?' Mum picked up the remote and started flicking through the channels.

'Oi, I was watching that! What do you mean? What have I done now?'

'You could have shown a bit more interest in how Charlotte got on!'

I stirred uncomfortably on the sofa next to Dad. 'Leave it, Mum, it's all right.'

'No, it's not all right!' Mum snapped at me as if I was in the wrong. 'It's always the same. I'm fed up with it.'

''Course I'm interested,' said Dad, putting his arm round me and giving me a squeeze. I could smell his breath, sour and beery. 'Charlie knows that, don't you, love?'

'Yes, Dad,' I said, trying to sound bored out of my mind. 'Whatever.' I wriggled away and pretended I was engrossed in the mindless game show on the screen.

'See, she's not bothered.' Dad took another swig at his pint and stretched his legs expansively. 'Rugby's for big ugly blokes like Will and me, not for pretty little things like our Charlie. Stands to reason you're not going to win with girls in the team. I mean, no girl, however skilled, is going to be as good as a boy, is she?'

'Typical! How do you work that one out?' spat Mum, curled up on her chair in a tight ball of fury.

'Where do I begin?' said Dad. He ticked off the reasons on his fingers.

'1. Boys are bigger.
 2. They've got more brute strength.
 3. They're better at—'

'It was a boy that lost them the game, flipping Wayne Dobson, dirty little player, not our Charlotte!'

'Well, there you are. Dirty play doesn't get you anywhere.' Dad stared morosely into his beer then drank deeply and, rubbing his hand across his mouth, continued, impervious to Mum's mounting rage. 'What do you want to play with the likes of him for? You don't want to play rugby, Charlie—'

'Well, that's where you're wrong, because that's exactly what she does want to do!'

'Look, I'm telling you, girls are not designed to play rugby and rugby was not designed for girls. They're a different build for goodness' sake, they're—'

'They're as good as boys, you just won't—'

'SHUT UP! SHUT UP, THE LOT OF YOU!'

I couldn't stand it any more. I'd looked forward to this day so much and it had ended in a free for all. I charged upstairs and into my bedroom, banging my door shut tight, and threw myself on my bed.

'Pretty little thing like Charlie.' That's all I'd ever be to him, a pretty little thing whose boobs got in the way of him ever taking me seriously. He'd never be proud of me, not like he was of Will, whatever I did.

I picked up my nail scissors and snipped at my hair where it was escaping from its ponytail in fine wisps round my face. That was better. I pulled the band out, shaking my hair free, and looked at myself in the mirror. No, it was worse. I didn't care.

I took the scissors and began to cut it, carefully at first, then, when I saw what a mess I was making of it, hacking it off in big savage clumps. When I finished I gasped at my reflection in the glass. I wasn't anyone's pretty little thing any more, that's for sure.

'Charlotte! What have you done!' Mum's screech brought Dad racing up the stairs. As he charged into my bedroom, she turned on him.

'This is all your fault! Yours and your flipping mother's!'

'What's my mother got to do with it?' asked Dad, staring at me aghast. 'Hell, Charlie, if you wanted a haircut, all you had to do was ask!'

Will's shocked face finished me off. I collapsed into Mum's arms and bawled my head off. She stroked my poor shorn head and rocked me like a baby, making soothing noises I remembered from my childhood.

When I calmed down she tucked me into bed.

'You know, nothing's ever this bad,' she said, smoothing my cheek. 'I'll tidy it up in the morning. It'll be fine.'

'Thanks, Mum.' I snuggled down under my duvet, feeling worn out. It had been quite a day.

In the morning Mum went off to the salon before I was awake and came back with her box of tricks. She started on my hair before I had time to look in the mirror and dissolve into tears again, banning Dad and Will from the kitchen.

First of all she washed it in her most expensive lemon-grass and lime moisturising shampoo, head back against the kitchen sink, as if I was in her salon. Then she gave me an Indian head massage. (Heaven! I was starting to enjoy this.) After that she got to work with her scissors, snipping and chopping, pausing every few minutes to muss it up, then back to work again. I almost expected her to ask me where I was going for my holidays but she was concentrating too much, tongue just visible between her teeth, a small frown between her eyebrows.

After what seemed an age, she put her scissors down with a sigh (of satisfaction? or desperation?) and picked up a jar.

'I'm going to use a definition wax and roughly blow-dry your hair. You won't have to do this if you don't want to. It's the sort of cut you won't have to fuss with.'

'Good,' I said. I really couldn't be bothered with messing about with my hair. I succumbed to Mum drying it which was actually very pleasant, warm and relaxing. At last she was finished.

'Ready?'

I nodded. It couldn't be worse, could it? She held up a hand mirror.

I didn't recognise myself. I'm not kidding. It was feathery and textured with short strands and longer layers on top. Mum had spiked up some bits and it looked cool. But it wasn't my hair that gave me the surprise. It was my face.

This face that stared back at me was nothing like the one I was used to. My eyes were much bigger and bluer for some reason and the shape of my face was different. Everything was more accentuated if you know what I mean. Now I knew what magazines meant when they said someone had a heart-shaped face.

'Do you like it?' asked Mum.

I nodded. I couldn't speak.

'It suits you. Shows off your cheekbones.'

'I look like Will.'

'Only prettier.'

It was true. I did look pretty. I grinned at Mum.

'I love it.'

She flung open the door.

'Will! Come in and take a look at your new sister!'

'Wow!' Will stared at me transfixed. 'You look amazing!'

'Dad?'

'It's lovely, sweetheart. You look a picture.'

'I can't believe how different you look,' said Will. 'You look older.'

'I do, don't I?' I turned my head this way and that. My neck seemed longer too. Weird. 'See, Mum, I told you I wanted my hair cut short, but you would never listen.'

'It's funny,' she said, admiring her handiwork. 'I thought it would make you look like a tomboy, but it doesn't. You look more feminine.'

'She was afraid you'd look like a dyke,' grinned Will.

I punched him. 'Just because you're gay . . .'

'He is not!' thundered Dad. 'My boy is NOT gay!'

'Da-ad!' said Will and I together.

Mum rolled her eyes and shook her head as she swept up my hair from the floor.

'For goodness' sake, Bob, give it a rest.'

Dad is so macho, it's pathetic. I wonder what he'd say if he knew what his pride and joy was up to.

I've discovered Will's little secret.

I'm amazed he's kept it to himself for so long. I never knew my brother could be so devious.

If it wasn't for Becky, I'd probably never have found out. You see, with all the fuss about me scalping myself on Saturday night, I forgot about the mystery of how he'd got to know Becky. Then she, as good as her word, texted me on Sunday and suggested we met up after school one day in the week. I'm not sure why, but I didn't mention it to Will. I guess I just wanted to get to know Becky better myself. After all, who wants their kid brother hanging around them all the time.

I said as much to Becky when she asked me where Will was. We were sharing a mango and peach smoothie at the Juice Bar in the shopping centre. She *loved* my hair, by the way.

'Dunno. At home I guess. He's not my shadow.'

'Pity. He's cool, your brother.'

'Will? He's just a kid.' I eyed her curiously. 'How do you know him anyway?'

'Stage Fright, I told you. Hey, Spider, you should come too. It's a real laugh.'

'Will goes to Stage Fright? Since when?'

'Not long. A couple of weeks. He's really good.' She sucked up the last of the drink, making farting noises and laughing as the woman next to us gave us a dirty look. Then her eyes grew serious. 'You didn't know, did you?'

I shook my head, feeling hurt. Since when had Will been doing things behind my back? And why hadn't Mum said anything? Then it dawned on me.

'What night is it on?'

'Friday. After school.'

So that was his little game. Mum hadn't mentioned it because she didn't know. And neither did Dad. Because as far as he was concerned, every Friday night after school, his son and heir, his pride and joy, was training for his debut match on the hallowed turf of the County Rugby Football Ground.

Instead of which William Webb-Ellis was turning into Billy Elliot.

And his father didn't have a clue.

I hate winter.

I hate the dark mornings when Mum has to drag me out of my bed for school and it still feels like the middle of the night and you've just closed your eyes.

I hate walking to school in the dark, especially when it's wet and the cars swish past and drench you with water from the puddles.

I hate it when you can't go out for hockey because it's raining and you're stuck in watching a video with seventy other kids who're not one bit interested so they mess about and you all end up in detention.

Then you don't just go to school in the dark, you come home in the dark as well.

The only things I like about winter are watching the Tinners play and Tag Rugby. But we're not playing Tag Rugby any more. Mr Brady gave us the good news and the bad news last week. He said, we'd have a Tag tournament again next year. Hurrah! But we don't need to practise again till next September. Rubbish.

The good thing is that Becky and I have become mates. I really like her. Most girls my age get on my nerves. They're so wet. All they do is hang round the boys, giggling and waiting to be asked out. But Becky's different. She's interested in boys, but *she* sets the agenda.

At the weekend we went to the home match together, Becky, Will and me. The Tinners lost, just. It was a good game though. I wore Craig's scarf, all nicely laundered by my mum and smelling of softener now, not sick, but he spotted me in it at half-time and I had to give it back. Dobbin came over with him and offered us chips and his own unique style of banal conversation, but I still hadn't forgiven him for losing us the tournament so I ignored him and chatted to Craig instead. He hung around though, scoffing chips and making daft conversation, and it was left to poor Becky to put up with him.

She did it in good part; I even heard her managing to giggle at some of his less crass comments. Luckily for her, once the game restarted he wandered back to the others.

Afterwards, Becky came back for a sleepover, my first blow-up mattress guest. Yay! I sprawled on my bed while she coloured her toenails green, then carefully painted white-petalled daisies on them. Then she did mine in white with red zigzags. England colours.

'That guy's a pain, isn't he?' she said, concentrating hard on my little toe.

'Who?'

'Keep still. The one with the chips.'

'Oh him. Dobbin. I thought you were getting on well.'

She straightened up and admired her handiwork. 'There, that'll do. What's his name?'

'Dobbin.'

'No, I mean his real name.'

'Wayne Dobson. Why?'

'Just wondered. He apologised to me, you know, for that daft tackle.'

'Did he?' I remembered how interested he was in Harry Roberts. 'I suppose he can be quite sweet at times.'

'Dobbin? Sweet?' Becky grinned at me. 'D'you fancy him?'

'Get lost!'

'You do, don't you?' There was a glint in her eye. I overreacted as usual, pretending to stick my fingers down my throat and make sick noises.

'Becky, he's minging. He's always been minging.'

She laughed. 'There you are, you're done. Don't smudge them.' She screwed the tops back on her bottles and put them away in her case. 'He's all right I suppose, quite nice-looking really. A bit immature, that's all.'

She was winding me up, trying to see if I really liked

him so she could set me up with him. I had to stamp on this quickly, before word got around.

'He's a geek,' I said firmly. 'A freak. A loser.'

She giggled. 'Los-er!' she echoed and then I felt mean. He wasn't that bad.

'Now your Will, he's going to be a stunner when he's older.'

I frowned. Was she serious? She'd better not get her claws into my brother no matter how good a mate she was.

'All the girls love him at Stage Fright,' she went on. I relaxed.

'You know he's missing rugby training to go to rehearsals, don't you? My dad'll go ballistic if he finds out.'

'He must really want to do it then.'

I nodded. That's what *he'd* said.

I'd spoken to Will about it after Becky had spilt the beans in the café that day. We were in his bedroom. There were more posters of musicals on the walls than rugby pictures now. Once he knew I wasn't going to dob him in to Dad he'd come clean.

'It's just something I want to do. I can't explain it. And now I've got the chance, I can't turn it down.'

'But you don't *like* being in the limelight. Look how embarrassed you were when you were clapped in assembly.'

He's nuts. I'd love it if the whole school clapped me.

He looked as baffled as I felt. 'I know. But it's different somehow. It's like it's not me up there on the stage, it's someone else. I forget about me and I concentrate on the character I'm playing and he takes over. I don't feel shy or anything.'

'How come you got in anyway? I thought you missed the auditions.'

'They couldn't find anyone for the male lead. I went back one day and they said I looked right for the part and could I sing? Once they heard me, they offered me the part there and then.'

'You kept that quiet!' I wasn't surprised. Will's got a great voice. The kind that reduces old ladies to tears.

'Yeah, well it was the same day the letter came from the RFU. And I'd just accepted the part and agreed to go to rehearsal every Friday night. I was so chuffed, Spider! I ran all the way home to tell you but then the letter was there waiting for me and I never got the chance to say anything about the musical; you were all so excited about the training sessions.'

I remembered that day. I couldn't work out at the time why he wasn't as pleased as we were.

His face shone. 'It's a brilliant show, Spi. It's set in the seventeenth century and it's sort of based on a true story. The black plague comes to a village and it's sealed off, so no one can get in or out. My girlfriend is stuck in there, that's Becky, so I try to break in to rescue her. It's all about the rescue attempt and what happens after. I'm not going to tell you, because I want you to come and see it.'

I nodded. It sounded good. 'Does Mum know what you're up to?'

He shook his head. 'She'd tell Dad.'

'You're going to have to tell him sometime.'

'I know, I know.' Then his face took on that closed-in expression. 'He'll stop me doing it.'

Dead right he will. For one thing, there's no way he'll allow him to miss rugby training for a match in which he's going to represent the County. And for another, he'll think Will's a wuss for wanting to go on the stage and sing and dance in the first place.

I could hear him now, 'What do you think you are? A flipping nancy boy?'

Because my dad, though I love him to bits and I'm sooo proud of him, and I'd do anything to make him proud of me – well, I have to admit, he's out of the Dark Ages. I could see where Will was coming from.

'But he's bound to find out sooner or later and then you'll be in deep trouble.'

'No he won't. The show's on before Christmas and the match isn't till the end of January. It'll all be over by then.'

He had it all worked out.

'So how come you've got off training so far?'

'I phoned up the number on the letter and told them I was ill.'

'Blimey Will, it's been weeks. What have you got, bubonic plague? Well, yeah, I suppose you have.' A ghost of a smile flitted across Will's face. 'It's not funny. They're going to be on to you soon, Will, asking questions. You'd better have a good story sorted.'

'I will, I will, I'll think of something. Just don't split on me, Spider, will you? Not to Mum or Dad, or Mr Brady either. Promise?'

I stared at him. This was the sort of mess I got into, not him. He was Mr Perfect, Mr Goody-Two-Shoes, Mr Never-Put-A-Foot-Wrong. If he was prepared to go to these lengths to do it, who was I to stand in his way?

'I promise.'

'So you're a rugby fanatic as well, Becky?' said Dad, as we were eating tea that night.

'I enjoy the game,' said Becky, tucking into Mum's lasagne.

'Your dad plays, does he?'

'I wouldn't know. I haven't seen him since I was three. He lives in Florida.'

Becky's so cool. She carried on demolishing her

lasagne while Dad sifted through his brain to find what to say next.

'So how did you get interested in the game then?'

'I played Tag Rugby at my primary school.'

'Lucky thing,' I said, reaching for the last piece of garlic bread to mop up my sauce. 'We played Towerball.'

Becky put down her knife and fork. 'Delicious.' She folded her arms on the table and sighed. 'Hey, Spider, I wish there was a women's rugby team we could join.'

I nodded gloomily. Life was peculiar. I'd give anything to play rugby and couldn't and here was Will tying himself in knots not to play.

'Start one,' said Mum, plonking steaming plates of apple tart and custard in front of us. Becky and I perked up.

'How?'

'I don't know. It can't be that difficult. Ask your dad.'

'Dad? How do you start a women's rugby team?'

He shrugged. 'Dunno. You'd have to find enough women to form a squad then find some mug who'd be willing to coach you, I suppose. You'd never do it.'

'Why not?' Three pairs of eyes stared accusingly at him. Will, who was keeping a low profile, kept his eyes on his apple tart.

'For a start, you'd never find that many women who'd be willing to play, let alone who'd be any good. And you'd never find a bloke brave enough – or daft enough – to take them on.'

'Who says?' Mum's eyes blazed at him. 'I wouldn't mind having a go.'

Will's spoon stopped in mid-air. I stared transfixed at Mum but at least I had the sense to keep quiet. Dad didn't though, he never learns. He burst out laughing.

'You must be joking!'

'No. Why do you think I'm joking?'

Oh no. Her voice had gone deadly quiet.

'Tracy, love, you've got to be fit to play rugby.'

'I could get fit.'

'How? You don't do anything!'

Dad, shut up, please.

'When do I have time to do anything? If I'm not in work I'm clearing up after you lot.'

'Don't give me that!' snorted Dad. 'You can't tell me you'd be out playing rugby if you had the chance.'

'I might be!'

'Give me a break. The most active thing you ever do is put your make-up on.'

'Blooming cheek! You're making me sound like a fat, lazy slob who sits on her backside all day!'

Becky finished her apple tart and studied her empty dish intently. Will slid off his chair and made for the door.

'You said it, not me!'

They were at it again. Mealtimes in the Webb-Ellis household. A peaceful exchange of interests and opinions.

'Anyway, how would you know what I get up to? You're never flipping here!' Once Mum gets going she can't stop.

Dad paused. 'We always knew I'd have to work all hours to get this business on the road,' he said quietly.

'Yeah, well don't tell me I'm a fat, lazy slob!'

'I never did!' Dad looked nonplussed. 'Charlie? Did I say your mother was a fat, lazy slob?'

'No, Mum, he didn't.'

Mum started grabbing the plates off the table and pitching them into the sink. She turned the hot tap on full and squirted washing-up liquid into the bowl. Water sprayed everywhere and bubbles rose alarmingly. She plunged her hands into the scalding water and yelped.

'Shit!'

Dad came over and turned off the tap. He took her hands and blew on them then wiped them gently with the tea-towel. Mum looked as if she was going to cry. Then he scooped up a handful of bubbles and carefully placed them on the end of Mum's nose.

'Idiot,' he said quietly.

'Pig!' she said back, but she flicked bubbles at him and giggled.

'It's all right, Will, you can come down now! They've stopped arguing!' I yelled up the stairs.

'Poor Becky. She must think she's landed in a mad-house,' said Mum. 'We're not always like this.'

'Yes we are,' I said. 'Come on, Becks, let's go upstairs.'

Later on, when Becky and I were in bed watching telly – well, I was in bed, Becky was on the mattress under my England bedspread which she'd pinched off me – Mum put her head around the door.

'Can I come in?'

I nodded, trying to swallow the sweet in my mouth and stuff the rest of the bag under the pillow before she could give me a lecture on oral hygiene. Becky, ignorant of Mum's little ways, popped another liquorice allsort in her mouth and offered her bag to Mum.

'No thanks, Beck. Budge up. Listen, you two. I've got a proposition for you.'

This sounded interesting. We turned the telly off and sat up.

'You know what we were talking about earlier . . .'

'You mean before or after the marital dispute?'

'Before . . . during . . . I don't know. Don't try to be clever with me, Charlotte. Listen. Do you both really want to play women's rugby?'

'Yeah.'

'Definitely.'

101

'Well then, I think we should start a team.'

'*We?*'

'Don't say it like that, Charlotte, you sound like your father. I'm serious. You must know some other girls who could play.'

'Well, yeah. There are a few girls from the tournament the other day we could get in touch with . . .'

'A couple of girls from my school might be interested,' put in Becky.

'Chloe and Freya at a push . . .'

'And I reckon I could round up some of my clients . . .'

'Mum, do you mean it?'

She nodded, eyes shining. 'Yes I do. I think we should go for it. Why should the men in this family get all the accolades? We'll show them what we're made of.'

'Yes!' I flung my arms round Mum then Becky did the same and we had a big group hug.

'What's going on in there?' came Dad's voice from the stairs. 'Get to sleep. Some of us have got work in the morning.'

We giggled and Mum put her finger to her lips. 'Don't say a word to him,' she said. 'Not till it's up and running. I don't want him saying I told you so if it all goes pear-shaped.'

'Okay.' More secrets in our family. Something occurred to me. 'Mum?'

'What?'

'Who's going to be our coach?'

'Don't you worry about that. I've got someone in mind. They might need a bit of persuasion, but I think they'll do it.' She got up off the bed and tucked us in. 'By the way, I'm planning to be in the team, so you'd better get used to the idea.'

Oh my word. Up to this point I thought she meant it all.

'Mum? Are you serious?'

'Charlotte,' she said, switching the light off and standing for a moment at the door, her figure, rounded and familiar, silhouetted against the landing light, 'I've never been more serious about anything in my life.'

Once Mum gets an idea in her head she wastes no time in acting upon it. She told Becky and me to put the feelers out on Monday at school. Stupidly I asked Chloe and Freya first and by lunchtime I had nearly all the girls in my year wanting to sign up, most of whom had never touched a rugby ball in their lives. I called a meeting on the school field.

'It's a women's rugby team,' I explained. 'You play against other women.'

'So we don't play against the boys?' asked Aisha, a tall skinny girl who squealed in horror every time the ball came near her in netball.

'No. Women play against women,' I said, gritting my teeth and assuming an expression of the utmost patience.

'Bor-ing,' said Aisha and got up to go. About half the group left with her.

'We'll need to train every week,' I continued.

'What sort of training?'

'Circuit training. Sit-ups, press-ups, squats, jogging, sprinting . . .'

More girls drifted off.

'Where do we train?'

'Not sure yet. Outside somewhere.'

'What happens if it's raining?' This came from Miranda, a girl with a permanent cold.

'What do you mean?'

'Do we still train if the weather's bad?'

'Of course we do. We train if it's cold, it's wet, it's snowing, if there's a blizzard. What's the weather got to do with it?'

'I hate going out in the rain . . .' Miranda sniffed and wandered off, followed by her cronies. Half a dozen girls remained.

'Do we have to come every week?' asked Freya. I eyed her balefully.

'Yes we do. And I expect you to go for a five-mile run in your own time too.'

There was a gasp and three more girls walked away. I was left with Chloe and Freya and a new girl I didn't know. She was tiny, even smaller than me, with fair hair tied into two thin plaits, and she clutched an asthma pump in her hand from which she kept taking surreptitious puffs. She looked about ten. I regarded her doubtfully.

'You up for this then?'

'Definitely.'

'I don't mean to be rude, but you have to be fit and strong to play rugby.' (Now who did I sound like?)

She grinned cheerfully. 'I know. I played before at my last school. Don't worry about this,' she waved her pump casually. 'It's just the move's upset my asthma. It'll calm down in a few days. I'm Janine by the way.'

'Nice to meet you. That's four of us then. I'll get back to you all when I've got more details.'

I hoped to goodness Becky and Mum had done better than I had.

It turned out Becky had done even worse. She had just one girl from her school, Crystal, who had probably only agreed to join because she was glued to Becky like a leech.

'She's quite a good athlete though and she's dependable. She should be okay.'

The next day Becky, Mum and I made up a list at home. We had another six definites we'd contacted from the Tag tournament, but it was Mum who'd scored. Marlene, her senior stylist, was up for it and nine clients had signed up from the salon, four facials, three leg-waxes and two bikini-lines.

'That's twenty-three all together, counting me,' said Mum, running her pencil down the list. 'No, twenty-four, I've forgotten Bev, my electrolysis.'

Enough to form a squad, counting the lady with a moustache. She could be useful in the front row.

The doorbell went. 'Get that, Charlotte.'

Phil Brady stood on the doorstep.

'Hello. It's not Thursday, is it?'

'I've been summoned. Is your mum in?'

The penny dropped.

'You're not . . . ?'

'Looks like,' he grinned. 'Your new coach. A very formidable lady, your mum. Does she ever take no for an answer?'

It was brilliant. We got so much sorted. Phil said to be honest he knew very little about women's rugby, but he'd find out how to set up a team. In the meantime we could use the school field for training on a Monday or a Friday night.

Will wandered into the kitchen while we were talking and picked up a book but I could tell he was listening to what was going on.

'How's the rugby training going, Will?' asked Phil.

'Okay,' Will grunted, not looking up from his book.

'I'll have to try and get up to see you after school one of these Fridays.'

Uh-oh! Will stirred uneasily, alarm bells pealing, and looked at me for help as usual.

'I thought we were meeting after school on Fridays for training?' I said.

'Or Mondays,' said Mum. 'Mondays are better for me. What about you, Becks?'

'Don't mind.'

'Mondays?' I said, thinking on my feet. 'That's a pity.'

'Why?' asked Mum.

'Miss Watkins is doing some extra French classes for those who are struggling. I thought I might go along and give them a whirl. Not to worry.'

'No, you must,' said Mum predictably. 'Fridays okay with you, Phil?'

'Perfect,' said Phil, giving me a questioning look. Too late, I remembered the graffiti on the sports hut wall that showed in explicit illustration the intimate relationship Mr Brady was engaged in with Miss Watkins. Oops. I wasn't such an accomplished liar as my little brother, was I?

I smiled innocently at Phil and, to my relief, he moved on to the boring admin side of setting up a new team. Will flashed me a look of gratitude. I'm amazed he's got this far without my help.

After a while Becky got up to go and Phil said he'd give her a lift as it had started raining. As they were leaving Dad walked in through the front door . . .

Dad's eyes opened wide in surprise as if he'd seen a

ghost and he said, 'Phil Brady! Well, I'll be blowed,' and Phil said, 'Hello, Bob. Long time no see.'

Mum asked, 'You two know each other then?' which was pretty obvious but instead of going into that hand-shaking, arm-punching, chuckling routine men normally do when they don't quite know what to say next they both stood there silent and finally Dad said, 'Aye, we go back a long way.'

'The rain's coming in,' I pointed out helpfully which gave Phil the excuse to move on out the front door with a 'We must catch up some time!' and a 'Yeah, yeah, we must do that' from Dad before he closed the door on Phil and Becky, rather precipitously I thought, and said, 'Fancy Phil Brady being Becky's dad. I thought she said he was in Florida.'

'He's not, you daft bat, he's Charlotte's new maths tutor.'

'Is he? Aye, well that makes sense, he was always a clever dick.'

'What's the connection between you two?' Mum took Dad's dinner out of the oven and put it on the table.

'Rugby.' Dad's voice was flat. 'What's he doing here anyway? I thought he came on Thursdays? We can't afford him twice a week.'

'It's all right. He just dropped some work off for our Charlotte.'

Since when did we all get to be such good liars in our family? Mum was at it now. 'Eat this up before it gets cold,' she said, without drawing a breath. 'It's your favourite, a nice bit of steak.'

Poor Dad. He never did get to finish his dinner that night. The phone rang and I went out to the hall to answer it. It was Granddad.

'Hello, Spider, love.' He stopped and gave a little cough. 'Is your gran with you by any chance?'

'Gran? No. Why?'

'Who's that?' called Mum from the kitchen.

'It's Gramps. He's asking if Gran is here.'

'No, don't trouble her . . .' he said, but it was too late. Mum took the phone and waved me away. I went back into the kitchen where Dad and Will were chatting as Dad tucked into his dinner. I ran some hot water into the bowl and squirted the washing-up liquid under the tap, wondering what was going on. Mum came back in looking worried.

'What's up?'

'Apparently Alice went out a couple of hours ago. She's not back yet.'

Dad looked up in surprise. 'Where did she go?'

Mum shook her head. 'That's the trouble. Joe doesn't know. She was in the kitchen clearing up after tea and he dozed off in front of the telly. When he woke up she'd gone.'

I looked at the window. Outside it was dark and rain splattered against the pane.

'Where the hell is she? Why did he let her go out on her own at this time of night? What's wrong with him?' Dad stood up and grabbed his car keys.

'What's wrong with her, you mean?' Mum muttered. 'He didn't *let* her, she just went. Wait for me, I'm coming with you.'

'No, you stay here, you never know, she might turn up. I'll take Charlie. Where do you think she's got to?'

'I don't know. She could be anywhere.'

Dad and I got in the van. He pulled out into the road, turning the windscreen wipers on and the heating up full blast.

Despite worrying about Gran, there was something nice and snug about being in the van in the dark, just the two of us, while the rain lashed down outside. Dad had asked me to go with him, not Will.

Then I got scared. Where was she? Surely she wasn't out on the streets in this?

'Where we going, Charlie? Where d'you think she's got to?'

'Maybe she's gone to see someone?'

'Who?'

'I dunno. She only comes to see us. Perhaps she's gone shopping?'

'At this time of night?' Dad shook his head, but nevertheless he turned the van towards town. I peered out through the windscreen at the driving rain, wondering where on earth Gran could have got to.

It had never occurred to me before, but really she didn't go far nowadays and hardly anywhere on her own. Not so long ago she used to be here, there and everywhere, dashing about, as Mum said, with a finger in everybody's pie. Now Granddad was always by her side. When was the last time she'd gone to see the Tinners play? I don't think she'd been this season.

Dad leant forward to wipe away the condensation on the windscreen. The streets were deserted, just the odd person hunched inside a raincoat, hands deep in pockets, head down against the incessant rain, another huddled under an umbrella, scurrying along the pavement. In the main street the shop windows cast forlorn pools of light on to the wet road. Apart from the Spar everything was closed. I got out and peered inside. There was no sign of her. Where was she?

At the far end, the big, square Georgian town hall stood solidly in darkness. About to get back in the van, I hesitated.

'What day is it?'

'Tuesday. Get in, Charlie, it's pouring.'

'Hang on a minute, Dad.'

Gran normally goes to Monday Club at the town hall. It's for senior citizens. They play bingo and have tea and biscuits and a chat.

Gran had a bit of a cold over the weekend. Mum said she didn't go to Monday Club last night.

I ran to the end of the road and sprinted up the steps. The big oak doors were tightly shut.

Huddled in the doorway, trying to shelter from the driving rain, was a tiny, bedraggled figure. I yelled to Dad.

'She's here!'

Dad leapt out of the van.

'What are you doing?' he yelled. 'You'll catch your death!'

Gran was drenched and shivering, her hair, usually in tight, neat curls, plastered tightly to her skull. Her best coat was saturated and she looked soaked to the skin. She clasped her handbag tightly to her like a shield.

I took her hand. It was freezing cold and I could feel the bones in it. It felt like a bird's wing.

'Come on, Gran. We'll take you home.'

She followed me as if she was a little girl and I was her mum. In the van she sat in the front and I squeezed in beside her and put my arms round her. She was wet through and shivering. Dad piled my coat and his on top of her and she put her head back on the seat and closed her eyes. Soon she was asleep. She hadn't said a thing.

Dad phoned Mum.

'Bring her here,' she said. 'I'll let your father know.'

At home Mum stood in the doorway waiting for us, a fidgeting silhouette against the yellow light. When Dad pulled up she ran out to help Gran from the van and took her straight upstairs into the bathroom. 'Put a hot water bottle in your bed, Charlotte,' she called downstairs. 'She can stay here tonight.'

When I brought the bottle up Mum was helping Gran into bed. It looked funny to see Gran in a big blue T-shirt nightie with a teddy bear on the front, but at least her cheeks were pink and her hair was dry and she looked more like herself. She even smiled at me and said, 'Hello, Spider, love, what are you doing here? You should be home in bed.'

Mum tutted. 'Sorry, love, but you'll have to go in with Will tonight. Put your blow-up mattress on his floor and use a sleeping bag. Say goodnight to your gran.'

I leant over and kissed her. She was warm now and smelt of Mum's best bath oil. 'See you in the morning, Gran.'

She patted my hand. 'You're a good girl,' she said. I felt a lump in my throat.

Downstairs Granddad had arrived and he and Dad

were at it. Granddad wanted to take her straight home.

'She'd be better off in her own bed,' he grumbled. 'You should have brought her straight home.'

'She was wet through and freezing cold,' said Dad. 'She needed warming up as soon as possible. Tracy knows what to do.'

'I can look after her,' said Granddad.

'I can see that!' snarled Dad. 'What do you think you're up to, letting her go wandering off on a night like this?'

'I didn't know she'd gone,' mumbled Granddad. 'She just went off without saying.'

'Did you have a row?'

'Of course not.' Granddad sounded impatient.

'She thought it was Monday. She was going to Monday Club,' I said. 'She didn't wander off. She got mixed up, that's all.'

'That's right, Spider, she got mixed up. Easy mistake to make.' Granddad looked at me gratefully. 'I'll take her home now. I'm sorry we've been such a nuisance to you.'

'You're not a nuisance,' said Mum, coming into the kitchen, carrying Gran's wet clothes. 'She's sound asleep now, Joe. Why don't you leave her where she is for the night? You go on home and get a good night's sleep and then you can collect her in the morning. Go on, you look done in.'

'I don't know . . .' Granddad looked tempted. 'She'll be fine,' Mum said decisively, pushing him gently towards the door. 'We'll look after her. I'll just put these on to dry then I'll put a drink of water by her bed in case she wakes up later.'

'No! Don't do that!' Granddad looked agitated. He turned to go upstairs.

'Look. I'd better take her now. I'll go and wake her up. She'll be all right.'

'Dad, she's not going anywhere,' said Mum, planting herself firmly in front of him and barring his way. 'And neither are you. Not until you sit down and tell us exactly what's going on.'

Poor Gran. Poor Gramps.

I'm never going to get old. I'm going to take a pill when I get to fifty.

I always thought being old was warm and cheerful. I thought it was coach trips and knitting patterns and a nice cup of tea.

I thought it was having a blue-rinse and getting tiddly at Christmas on one too many sherries or that funny yellow drink called a snowball.

I thought it was collecting your pension on a Monday and spending it on bingo and a flutter on the horses and treats for the grandchildren.

Well, it's not. Those are clichés. It's not like that at all.

It's not remembering who you are and where you live and what day of the week it is.

It's getting mega cross with yourself and everybody else when you get mixed up.

It's forgetting how to do things you've always done without thinking. Like going to the toilet. And washing your clothes. And keeping yourself clean.

I don't want to go on.

You know the really awful, dreadful thing? When Mum stood in front of Granddad that night with her arms folded and demanded to know what was going on, do you know what he did? He started crying.

He didn't cry like Will does, silently and soulfully, with huge tears spilling from his eyes and rolling down his cheeks. He didn't cry like I do, bawling and gulping and spitting out words of fury.

He made a deep, rasping, painful sound, as if he couldn't breathe properly, then his shoulders shook. He sat down on the first step, clutching his head in his hands, then made the same sound, louder this time, as if he was tearing it up from somewhere deep inside. At first I thought he was having a heart attack. Then I saw his face was wet.

Mum sat down on the step next to him and put her arm round him. She said, 'It's okay, it's okay,' and looked up at Dad in alarm. He was staring at Granddad, horrified, and he said, 'What's up, mate?' but Mum shook her head and took Granddad's hand in hers. Will, looking white, went into the lounge and shut the door. I chewed my nails and wondered what to do.

After a while Granddad's shoulders stopped heaving and he pulled his hanky out of his pocket and wiped his eyes then he blew his nose hard. He breathed a big, final, shuddering sigh then he looked up at me and tried a smile.

'Sorry, Spider love.'

'You all right, Gramps?'

He closed his eyes. Don't cry again, I begged silently.

'Nothing that a nice cup of tea won't put right.' He stood up and patted Mum on the arm. 'Looks like I've got some explaining to do.'

We went into the lounge and Granddad sat in the chair by the fire. I perched on the arm beside him.

'Give Granddad some space,' said Mum, handing him a cup of tea. I went to move but Granddad said, 'No, stay where you are. You might as well hear this.'

'What's wrong with Gran?' My voice sounded frightened even to me. 'She's not going to die, is she?'

'No my love, she's not going to die.' Granddad squeezed me tightly and relief flooded through me.

'She's just become very forgetful recently,' he continued. 'She gets confused about what she's meant to be doing.'

Was that all? What on earth was all the fuss about?

'So? Mum's always forgetting things,' I said. 'You forgot to iron my school shirt at the weekend, didn't you, Mum, and I had to go to school with it all creased.'

'That's different,' said Mum shortly. 'That's because I've got too much to do. Anyway, you're old enough to iron your own shirt. Go on, Joe.'

Granddad slurped his tea slowly then he put his cup down on the table.

'I've noticed it for a while. She gets the days of the week mixed up. And she's not as . . . fussy . . . as she used to be. The time was you could eat your dinner off our kitchen floor, it was so clean. Now she doesn't put a mop over it from one month to the next. And cooking? You know what a good cook she was.'

Mum nodded. Hypocrite!

'Well, now it's as if she's forgotten what to do. She forgets to put salt in the potatoes and when I tell her she puts sugar in instead.'

Will chuckled and I scowled at him.

'So what? Who cares about boring old housework anyway? Gran remembers all the important stuff. She can tell you every member of the Olympic team from 1908, can't she, Dad?'

Dad nodded. 'Charlie's right. Mum can remember who won the County Championship going back to the beginning of the last century. There's nothing wrong with her memory.'

'It's not the things that happened a long time ago,'

said Granddad. 'It's the day-to-day stuff she forgets. Like getting dressed in the morning . . . and keeping herself clean.' He cast a sidelong glance at Will who developed a sudden interest in the back page of yesterday's newspaper. 'She's not as . . . fastidious as she used to be.'

I recalled the last time Gran had babysat for us. The smell of wee. My heart sank.

'Have you taken her to the doctor?' Mum asked, leaning forward and taking his hand in hers. He shook his head.

'She won't go. What can you do?'

Mum sighed. 'She needs to see a doctor. It's probably nothing, but she should be checked out. Don't worry, Joe, I'll speak to her. Now you go on home and have a good night's sleep and everything'll seem much better in the morning.'

Dad let Granddad out and came back into the lounge rubbing the back of his neck.

'He's making a fuss about nothing,' he said. 'Poor old bird, she just went out on the wrong night and got caught in the rain. The way he's going on you'd reckon she was doolally.'

Mum gave him a withering look. 'Sometimes,' she said, 'you can be incredibly stupid.' Then she noticed me taking it all in and said, 'Bed! You've got school in the morning.'

Huh! Those words will be engraved on my tombstone.

The next morning, after a night spent listening to Will's snuffles (I've got used to being on my own, it's not fair!) my bedroom door remained firmly closed.

'I need my school uniform!' I wailed at Mum.

'Go on in and get it then!' she hissed. She was on the phone trying to get hold of one of the other stylists to open the salon for her. 'Don't disturb her though.'

I pushed the door open quietly. The room was in darkness, just a lump in the bed snoring gently. I tiptoed over to my wardrobe where my uniform was hanging, then fished around in my drawers for a clean pair of knickers and socks. I couldn't see a thing. I debated turning on the light but Gran did a colossal snore and turned over. I froze.

There was a funny smell in the room. Like wet nappies. Like wee. It was wee. I felt sick.

Downstairs, Mum put down the phone.

'What's the matter? Is your gran all right?'

I nodded.

'What's up then?'

'She's wet the bed.'

'What?'

'Gran's peed in my bed.'

Mum closed her eyes. 'Is she awake?' I shook my head.

'Don't worry then, I'll sort it.' She ran her hand

through her hair. 'I'll never get to work today. You'd better get off to school.' She gave me a quick kiss. 'She can't help it, Charlotte.'

'I know that.' What was wrong with Gran? How could she? It was disgusting. I don't want to sleep in my bed ever again.

School was okay, better than home at the moment, anyway. Since I'd been having coaching from Phil I was finding maths a lot easier. We were doing Number and for once I was ahead of the game. Phil had been showing me how to multiply and divide fractions and I tore through the workbook, finishing before everyone else. I took it out to old Dale the Fail to be marked and I got them all right. It was worth every penny of Dad's hard-earned money to see his face.

'Well, well, well,' he said, sourly, putting the minutest tick in the corner of the page. Huh! If they were wrong he would have slashed the page with his red biro. 'Wonders will never cease.'

No thanks to you, I thought, and made out I didn't give a stuff, but secretly I was thrilled to bits. Like a little kid with a gold star.

He called Dobbin out next to mark his book. Well he would, wouldn't he, being as he'd missed out on unleashing his venom on me. Of course, Dobbin knew he was going to get them all wrong, I mean he hadn't had the benefit of the Brady Kid's help, so he played for time, pretending not to hear his name being called and that got Dale's back up straight away. By the time Dobbin had finally sauntered out to him, looking as if he didn't have a care in the world and dropped his book on the desk unopened, Greaseball Dale was ready to tear him to shreds.

He was dying to tell him to open his book at the correct place but he didn't dare in case Dobbin refused. Even from where I was sitting I could see beads of sweat breaking out on his forehead. Instead he snatched up the book and rifled through it till he found the right page then went into that defence of all rubbish teachers, sarcastic mode, making out that his Year 7s were brighter than Dobbin.

'Dear me, dear me,' he drawled, shaking his head and pretending concern. 'What are we going to do with you, Wayne? Maybe you should go back to Year 7 and start again.' He scored his book heavily with his evil pen and went for the cheap laugh. 'Or maybe we could arrange to send you down to the infants' school.'

It worked. A titter went round the classroom; I mean, you couldn't help picturing Dobbin, all arms and legs, perching there on one of those tiny chairs in the middle of a class full of little kids. He'd be like Gulliver or the BFG only it would be the BUG in his case (Big Unfriendly Giant).

Well, Dobbin wasn't going to stand there and take that, was he?

'I'm not thick,' he growled. 'I just can't be arsed.' This got a cheer and a round of applause from the class and Dale went puce and said, 'That's a matter of opinion' and slapped a detention on him for using obscenities. One or two people behind me sniggered and I turned around and told them to shut up.

Poor Dobbin. He swaggered back to his seat clutching a detention slip and making out he didn't give a toss but I knew what he was feeling like inside. Moronic. It's not a pleasant feeling.

I can't believe I said that. Poor Dobbin.

The weird thing was, as I improved at maths it seemed to spill over into other subjects. I was getting better at everything, even French, which was just as well because Mum thought I was having extra classes on a Monday. For years I hadn't tried at school because I was convinced I was no good at anything (except for sport, which I didn't have to try at). It was like, from the minute I walked into secondary school there had been a row of big locked doors in front of me labelled Maths, English, Science, French, Humanities, etc., which I couldn't get through. (I don't know why, I can't remember being thick at primary.) Now someone had handed me the key to the maths door and I found that it opened all the others too.

That someone was Phil Brady.

At lunchtime I knocked on the staff-room door.

'Can't you read that notice?'

Too late I saw the DO NOT DISTURB sign.

'Emergency, Miss,' I explained glibly. 'Is Mr Brady there?'

Phil appeared frowning, sandwich in his hand.

'What's up?'

'Can I borrow a rugby ball, Sir?'

'Bloody cheek,' he growled but he tossed his bunch of keys to me. 'Help yourself and lock the cupboard after you.'

I rounded up Janine, Chloe and Freya and we collected a ball from the stock cupboard in the gym and went out on to the field. We started running up and down, passing the ball to each other, and within minutes we'd attracted the attention of the boys from our year. They stood around, jeering at first, then Craig said, 'Want a game?'

'If you like.'

We divided into two teams, Janine and me going with Nathan and Gavin, Chloe and Freya with Craig and Dobbin. We played across the field with our school jumpers for goalposts. Immediately Janine made the quickest try on record, picking up the ball from me and flying down the outside to place it neatly between the posts.

'I wasn't ready!' protested Freya but we shouted her down and by the time she'd shut up, Gavin had done it again. Then the opposition got their act together with a run and kick set-up between Chloe and Craig, technically terrible but it worked. Chloe's face when she touched down was a picture. Craig scored again then Dobbin topped it off to run straight through me for the winning try. The bell rang and we were beaten, three tries to two.

'That was all right,' said Dobbin as we walked off the field. 'Give you a game tomorrow?'

'Yeah,' I said, a bit grumpy at being pipped to the post. 'Whatever.' He wouldn't be asking if he'd lost. He sounded almost human for once. Maybe Neanderthal Man was evolving after all this time.

As Dobbin bent down to pick up his bag, his maths book fell out. He swore and stuffed it back in and when he stood up his face was red.

'Thanks, by the way,' he said.

'What for?'

'Sticking up for me in maths. When Dale was having a go at me.'

'Oh him! He's a pillock.'

'Yeah he is. A prize pillock.'

'A first-class, number-one, prize pillock.'

Dobbin grinned and his face lit up. He looked nice when he smiled.

He slung his bag over his shoulder and said 'See you then,' and ambled off. I watched him for a while then I yelled out, 'A premier-division, first-class, number-one, prize pillock!' and he turned round and waved.

I heard a giggle behind me. Freya and Chloe were hanging round each other's necks making kissy-kissy noises, then they broke into a chant of,

'Spider and Dobbin, sitting in a tree,
K-I-S-S-I-N-G!'

I made an extremely rude gesture at them and they burst out laughing.

When I got home that afternoon, the house was full. Gran and Granddad were in the sitting room watching telly with Will, and Mum was busy ironing in the kitchen.

'They still here?'

'Staying for tea and then they're off home.'

'Is Gran okay?'

Mum swept the iron deftly into the shoulders of Dad's shirt. Steam rose.

'Seems back to normal today. She hasn't said a thing about last night, I think she's forgotten all about it. Best not to mention it.'

My England bedspread and my bed sheets lay neatly folded in the ironing pile. She saw me looking at them.

'Don't worry. I've changed your bed. No harm done.'

'Why does she do that?' My nose wrinkled. Mum

129

slipped Dad's shirt on a coat hanger and hung it on the back of the door.

'She's getting old. She can't help it.'

'She's not that old.'

'No.' Mum sighed. 'Go and set the table for me, Charlotte, there's a good girl.'

I took the knives and forks into the dining room, tablecloth under my arm. It's really all one big lounge with the sitting room at one end and the dining table at the other. When it's just us we eat around the kitchen table but if we have company Mum insists on the dining table with a cloth and napkins then complains about having to wash them.

'Hello, Spider, love,' said Gran, normal as can be. 'Had a good day at school?'

'Yes thanks, Gran. What you watching?'

'I don't know. There's nothing much on nowadays.' She got up out of the chair. 'I'll give you a hand.'

I gave her the cloth and the knives and forks and went out to get the drinks. When I came back in she was standing gazing out of the window at the back garden, arms folded. The cloth and cutlery lay in a heap on the table.

'All right, Gran?' I asked.

'Yes thanks, love,' she said and went and sat back down next to Granddad. He looked up at me and sighed, eyebrows raised. I laid the table.

After dinner I went up to my bedroom to get on with my homework. I inhaled deeply but I couldn't smell a thing. I hate to say it but I even got down on my knees and sniffed the mattress. Nothing, just the flowery aroma of Mum's softener. Thank goodness for that!

I was deeply into my English homework when Will came to find me. It doesn't sound like me, I know, but it's ace. We've been learning about writing for different purposes, like formal letters, newspaper articles, posters, memos, etc. and we have to use them all for one topic. Miss is going to make a display of them at Parents' Evening. Chloe, Freya, Janine and I are doing ours on rugby!

Tonight I was working on the poster. People don't realise how important words are in posters. It's a bit like poetry – the right words in the right order. And they've got to catch your eye. I'd cut up words on bits of paper and was moving them around on the page like a jigsaw when I noticed Will standing at my door clutching a big piece of paper. He was looking worried.

'What's up?' I asked.

'Look!' He thrust the paper in front of me. It was a poster, much brighter and shinier and more professional than the one I was doing. And it had my best mate's and my little brother's faces beaming out of it. It was an advert for the Christmas musical at the town hall.

'Wow, Will, that's amazing,' I breathed. I looked at the title of the musical and giggled. *A Plague on Your Town*, it was called. 'Not very Christmassy, is it?'

'Look what it says.' He pointed to the print underneath,

'Starring Becky Martin and William Webb-Ellis,' I read aloud. 'Lucky things. You've got your name in lights.'

'They're going to put them up soon,' he said, his voice peculiarly flat and toneless. 'They'll be in the library, in the town hall, in school. They even asked me if Mum would be willing to put one in the salon window.'

'You bet she would. She'd be made up.' Why wasn't he excited? I'd be over the moon if it were me with my name plastered all over town for everyone to see.

And then I remembered. She didn't know anything about it, did she?

And neither did Dad.

'Oh shit. You've got to tell them, Will.'

'I know! I *am* going to!' He sounded desperate. 'But what with all the fuss about Gran, I haven't had a chance.' He flung himself down by my bed and clasped his knees to his chest, staring moodily at the floor.

'I can't understand how you've got away with it up to now. It's a wonder the RFU haven't notified the school.'

There was silence. I stared at him.

'What have you done?'

He shifted uncomfortably.

'Nothing.'

'Will!'

'All right! I wrote a letter to them.'

'You did what? What did you say?'

'I pretended I was Dad. I said my son had been in hospital and would need to recuperate but he'd be fit to start training again after Christmas.'

'You never!' He wasn't even twelve yet! I mean, I know he's bright but that's ridiculous! 'How did you know what to say?'

'We were doing formal letters in English and we had to do one for homework. So I wrote one to the RFU. Look, I'll show you, I got it marked!'

He disappeared into his bedroom and came back brandishing his book. His letter had been corrected in pencil by his nice young English teacher with suggestions for layout and vocabulary (no savage Dale the Fail red pen for her) and it had an 'A for effort and originality. Well done, Will!' in the margin. Trust Will!

'So then I typed it out again on Dad's business notepaper, and sent it off to them.'

'What did they say?'

'Sorry to hear I'd been ill, hope I'd be better soon, they'd keep my place in the team, all that sort of stuff. They were really nice about it.'

'That's a real con, Will. You should be ashamed of yourself.'

'I know, I am. I really am.' At least he had the grace to look embarrassed. 'But there's no harm done. Dad won't know anything about it because he can't come and watch me training, he's too busy at work. And this way, I get to do the show *and* keep my place in the team. So no one loses out.'

I stared at Will, awestruck. Who would have thought my law-abiding little brother had it in him? It was wrong what he was doing, I know that, but I couldn't help admiring him. I mean, it took some nerve to pull the wool over everyone's eyes.

Like Becky said, he must really want to do it.

Will had a reprieve, for the time being at least. They decided not to put the posters up till the first week of December. He looked as if he had the weight of the world lifted from his shoulders. I would've thought he'd be worried about what would happen then, but Will doesn't seem to be operating like that any more. It's like he's dealing with what's going on now and letting the future take care of itself. He never used to be like that; this blooming show has changed him. It's me who's doing all the worrying!

'You've got to tell Dad,' I reminded him on a daily basis but, to be fair, it was impossible. We hardly saw him over the next few weeks, he was so busy at work and I mean, it's not exactly the sort of thing you can throw into the conversation without a Third World War breaking out, is it? 'Oh, by the way, Dad, I've decided not to play rugby for the County for the time being,

I'm more into tap dancing now.' Not with a father like ours, anyway.

Dad has got a big new contract with Scotts who are building a block of flats near the docklands where all the redevelopment's taking place. They've subcontracted the kitchens and bathrooms to him. He's had to take on new staff and another loan to pay their wages.

'You've got to spend money to make money,' he said to Mum when she asked if he knew what he was doing. He went out early in the morning before we got up and didn't get home till late at night. I think he got into the habit of stopping off at the pub on his way home with the new blokes he'd taken on because Mum had a go at him about it one Sunday.

'There's not much point in working all hours of the day and night to make a success of this business if you're going to drink all the profits.'

Dad scowled. 'You begrudge me a quick drink now? I'm putting in twelve-hour days and it's hard graft, Tracy. I don't sit around painting women's nails all day, you know. I'd like to see you digging foundations and lugging bricks.'

I giggled at the thought of Mum down a hole in a hard yellow hat while Dad, wearing a white, tight-fitting little number, perched on a stool and buffed nails with an emery board, but Mum's face was like thunder. I don't blame her. I've seen how hard she works in that salon, on her feet all day.

'You're never here,' she said, pulling the chicken out of the oven and poking it with a fork. Juices ran spitting into the roasting dish. She spooned them over the potatoes, splashing hot fat on her hand in the process. 'Damn,' she said, sucking her fingers. 'And when did you last see your mother?'

'What's this, the Spanish Inquisition? She's coming round for her dinner today, isn't she?'

'Only because I bothered to ask her. If it were left to you we'd never see her from one month to the next. And while we're on the subject, when did you last kick a football round with the kids? Or go and watch Will training?'

Will stared fixedly at the gas fire. Oops, Mum, don't go down that path.

Dad looked at us guiltily. 'I'll make it up to you, I promise. I'll get to see you train before Christmas, Will. I'm just so busy at the minute.'

'It's all right, Dad, you're not missing much. We'll be doing more in the New Year.' Will avoided my eyes.

'Not doing much? You should be well into it by now. What drills are you up to?'

Will stared at me desperately.

'You're doing Smart skills aren't you, Will?' I prompted.

'What's that when it's at home?' asked Dad.

The front doorbell rang. Will jumped up in relief.

'Gran and Granddad are here! I'll get them!' There was a lot of greeting and kissing and hanging up of coats and clearing away of the Sunday papers so everyone could sit down and by the time we were all settled in the lounge with a cup of tea Dad had forgotten all about rugby training.

'How you keeping, Alice?' asked Mum.

'Fine, thank you,' said Gran. 'Mustn't complain.' She looked nice today; she'd had her hair done and she was wearing a pretty pink jumper and her best black skirt with a swirly pattern on. 'Come and sit by me, Spider.' She patted the sofa next to her. I sat down between her and Granddad and breathed in cautiously. She smelt of soap and talc. I smiled at her and she stroked my cheek with the back of her hand.

'You're getting bonnier every day,' she said. 'Who'd have thought it?'

'Gran!' Was that her idea of a compliment? Everyone laughed, though Granddad tutted. I glanced at him. His hands were resting on his knees, large veins running between a pattern of sunspots. On his wrist he wore the gold watch he'd been given by the management when the tin-mine he'd worked in all his life closed down. I traced the face of the watch with my finger and he smiled, trapping my finger under his thumb.

'That's for you one day,' he whispered.

'Not Will?' I whispered back.

He shook his head. 'We'll find something else for him.'

'He'll get the silver medal,' I said wistfully. Granddad patted my hand. His skin felt dry and crinkled like parchment. Close up it struck me he actually seemed older and less robust than Gran, for all his size. He looked grey, not just his hair but his skin, and he had dark circles under his eyes as if he hadn't slept. As if Mum was reading my mind she said, 'You okay, Joe? You're looking tired.'

'He's not sleeping,' said Gran, bright as a button. 'He was up and down all night like a yo-yo.'

'I was trying to get you back to bed! She suddenly decided she wanted to spring-clean the house at three o'clock this morning!'

Gran looked surprised at his outburst. 'No I didn't!' She turned to Mum and laughed. 'Don't believe a word he says. He's making it up.'

Granddad shook his head wearily at Mum. I slipped my hand into his and gave it a squeeze. I knew who was telling the truth.

Granddad sighed. 'Now then, what's happened to this dinner? We're starving, aren't we, Spider?'

Mum dished out the dinner. It was yummy, roast chicken and spuds, soaked in gravy, with swede and carrots mashed together, just how I like them, and baby sprouts from Granddad's allotment. I'm weird, I love sprouts.

We all polished off our plates, except for Granddad. Considering he'd just said he was starving, he didn't seem to have much of an appetite. He gave Will his chicken leg and just took a small piece of breast instead and he left half his vegetables, even his roast potatoes. He even said, 'Not for me,' when Mum offered him bread and butter pudding for afters, with clotted cream.

'It's your favourite,' Mum said, but he shook his head. Gran didn't seem to notice, she was too busy licking the cream off her spoon, but Mum looked a bit worried.

When they'd gone she said to Dad, 'Your father's not right, you know, he's got no appetite. He's worn out keeping an eye on Alice.'

'Here she goes,' said Dad, stretching out on the sofa and flicking the telly on with the remote. 'You've always got to have some thing to worry about lately. It was my mother you were going on about a few weeks ago. There's nothing wrong with her and there's nothing wrong with my father. They're just getting on a bit, that's all.'

'How would you know? You wouldn't notice if your parents sold up and went backpacking. Come on, Charlotte, we're going for a walk.'

She slammed the roasting tin back into the cupboard and chucked the tea-towel in the wash. In the porch we put our trainers on and went out into the cold clear air.

'I'll swing for him one day,' she said, but she looked better already. For the past few Sundays we'd got into the habit of going for a run in the afternoon. As far as Dad was concerned we were going for a walk in the park, but in reality we were slowly building up our fitness in a strict programme set up for us by Phil.

I was surprised at Mum. We'd started by running one minute, then walking one minute. 'I can't do this,' she'd gasped, holding her side, 'I've got a stitch.' But she'd persevered, going out for a run every day in her lunch hour until the next Sunday she could manage three minutes without stopping. Now she was up to ten minutes and getting faster all the time, even though Phil had said speed wasn't important, it was stamina we needed to build up. Until now I'd had to slow down my pace to hers. Today we were running together, matching stride for stride.

'You're good, Mum. You've really come on.'

She stuck her thumb up in acknowledgement and we ran across the park together stretching out comfortably. At the lake we slowed down to a walk and made our way along the path at the water's edge, avoiding the mums pushing buggies and the kids on bikes.

'What's this, a go-slow?'

We turned at the sound of a familiar voice. Phil was behind us, arm in arm with Miss Watkins. She looked younger out of school with her hair down round her shoulders. Mum broke into a smile.

'I can do ten minutes now with a minute's rest in between.'

'Not bad. Wish they were all as dedicated as you.'

'Oh, they're coming on,' said Mum, squinting up at him in the watery sun. 'The young ones especially.'

Phil nodded. 'I've got all the stuff through from the RFU. We need to go through it together sometime this week.'

Mum nodded. 'No problem.' She turned to Miss Watkins. 'How are the French classes?'

Miss Watkins looked puzzled. 'Fine,' she said, obviously having no clue whatsoever to which French classes Mum was referring. No wonder. It was the extra French classes on a Monday night. The ones I'd made up. Oops.

'They've made such a difference to our Charlotte,' gushed Mum.

Miss Watkins looked baffled. Phil looked amused. I looked at my watch.

'Come on, Mum, I've got homework to do.' I tugged urgently at her arm.

'You see? She's so keen nowadays,' said Mum, but

luckily she followed me, leaving Miss Watkins staring after her. 'Wonder what he sees in her?' she said. 'She seems pretty gormless to me.'

'Gormless,' I repeated. 'She's got no gorm.' We burst out laughing and broke into a run.

Back at home Dad was fast asleep on the sofa snoring his head off, the television blaring away. Upstairs, Will was going through his lines.

'Test me, Spider,' he said, thrusting the script into my hands.

'You haven't told him, have you? You could have told him while Mum and I were out.'

'He's been asleep!'

'Excuses! You are going to be in so much trouble when they find out. Mum nearly blew it earlier on when she told Dad to go and watch you training.'

It was getting too complicated. I hated the way everyone in this family was keeping secrets from each other. It was hard to keep track of who knew what. I'd said to Mum the other day, 'When are we going to tell Dad about our team?' and she'd said, 'When I'm good and ready and not before.' I think she wants to make sure it's really going to happen so he can't turn round and say, 'I told you so,' if it all goes wrong.

And it *is* going to happen, only not exactly as we'd first

imagined it. For a start, there isn't going to be *a* women's rugby team – there are going to be two! Phil had got on to the RFU and discovered that there were age restrictions. My mates and I would be playing as Under Fourteens while Mum and her clients would be Seniors.

'But there won't be enough of us,' said Mum looking worried. 'We've only got twenty-four all together.'

'That's okay for the time being,' said Phil. 'We'll train as two teams of twelve playing against each other. Then, when it's time to organise fixtures, we can play with restricted numbers. We'll need to set up a committee too.'

So every Friday evening for the past month or so, in all sorts of weathers, we'd turned out on the school field for training. What a motley crew we were! All shapes and sizes from Marlene, Mum's Amazonian stylist, to teeny-weeny Janine.

Each time we met, Phil put us through a fitness programme to increase our strength and stamina, then we practised techniques and finally we played a game, ten minutes each way. The fitness was hard, the drills were fun and the matches . . . well, they got better as the weeks went on.

Phil's a good coach. He had a battle on his hands at the start; he must have wondered what on earth he'd got himself into. I mean Becky, Janine and I, and the other girls who'd played Tag Rugby, at least we had some idea what we were supposed to be doing. But the next level, like Crystal, Chloe and Freya and one or two of Mum's clients, even though they were reasonably fit and up for it they were clueless as far as rugby was concerned.

And then there were the rest. Women like Marlene whose idea of keeping fit was standing on the scales at Weight Watchers, who watched the Wimbledon Final on telly and felt exhausted, who had their highlights done each week before they came. (Or in Bev's case, her moustache.) Mind you, Becky's the same. I don't mean she has her tash done because she hasn't got one (yet) but she does overdo the personal grooming if you ask me.

The first session was a hoot. First of all we ran twice around the field. Well, some of us did. Marlene ('I was really good at running at school!') went like a bat out of hell and collapsed in a heap, gasping for air, after the first hundred metres. Most of the oldies failed to make the second lap. After that we went into a stretch routine which people coped with on the whole though they grumbled a lot. The strength exercises defeated everyone including me. I'm sure there's a biological reason why women can't do press-ups.

We didn't even make it to a game that first night, most

of the squad being too knackered. They perked up afterwards though, especially the oldies. Phil had arranged that we could use the school changing rooms and once they'd stripped off and were in the showers, they got down to business.

Ironically, the Under Fourteens nipped in and out of the shower pretty quickly, including Becky who normally loved any opportunity to cleanse and pamper. I think we were all a bit overawed by the sheer volume of female flesh on display. But those older women were into serious grooming: well, I guess it's to be expected, they are Mum's regular clients after all.

They went into those showers armed with every cleansing product under the sun – shampoos, shower gels, conditioners, body scrubs, lotions, serums, mud packs, body brushes, exfoliators, you name it, there it was, bursting out of their packed wash bags. They must have torn through Boots and Superdrug like a hurricane, leaving shelves stripped bare.

I'll tell you something, in between the cleansing and polishing I'd never heard conversations like it this side of those confessional TV shows you catch when you're off school on a weekday morning. No subject was taboo. Pre-menstrual tension, the menopause, troublesome teenage children, faulty husbands, divorce, breast enlargement, breast reduction, liposuction, sex — you name it, they discussed it, in strident voices and shrieks of laughter, except for sex which, thank goodness, was discussed in whispered undertones. It was hilarious and a real education for us Under Fourteens, I can tell you — though a tad embarrassing to hear your own mother pontificating on the virtues of one sort of bikini wax over another. (Mind you, she is a beautician).

And talking of bikini waxes, when they finally came out, pink and steaming and wrapped in bright-coloured towels, Marlene sporting a particularly fetching orange velour number which clashed rather with her crimson plastic shower cap, all was not over, not by a long chalk. Now new bags were opened and out came the waxing kits, the epilators, and the other fuzz busters along with the anti-cellulite gels. I don't want to go into this in any depth, wax virgin that I am — suffice to say that Bev's moustache is not the full extent of her prolific hair problem and her dealing with it led Chloe, Freya and Janine to beat a hasty retreat while Becky watched spellbound, on a steep learning curve.

'Bev says the secret of the bikini-line blitz,' she informed me earnestly the next day, 'is in the diluted tea-tree oil which prevents irritation and stinging and soothes sensitive areas.'

Puh-lease!

Even Becky drew the line when Marlene, in her underwear, decided to demonstrate the pert bottom squat. Interestingly, pert is an adjective I would never have associated with Marlene. We both watched with horrible fascination as she took a deep breath, drew her belly in (marginally), bent her legs and slowly and deliberately squatted down, thighs parallel to the floor, bum stuck out behind her. That was enough for us. We didn't wait to see if she ever got up again but charged outside, holding our sides, as our screams of laughter erupted into the clear night air.

But here's the thing, only a few weeks on and what a difference in their fitness. Phil gave us an exercise sheet to follow in our own time and by and large people have been pretty good at sticking to it. Couple that with going for a run a few times a week and everyone's improved. You don't notice it so much in the youngsters but in the Seniors it's visible. They're all that bit more toned, that bit faster, that bit more flexible. And to tell the truth, I'm proud of them.

'Sod the diet!' Mum groaned on her way home last Friday. 'Who needs to cut calories when you've got this blooming ball to chase around.'

By the time we got home Will was invariably back from rehearsal (or training as far as Mum was concerned). She always went straight to run a bath and lay soaking in the bubbles, sipping a glass of wine until she fell asleep and I had to wake her by tapping on the door, so he got away without a cross-examination. And then when Dad eventually made it home from the pub where he'd been quenching his thirst after a long week's work, we were all safely tucked up in bed.

So I guess that's how Will's got away with it for so long.

He's good, my little brother, very good. Even as he went through his lines parrot-fashion to make sure he'd got them word-perfect, I felt a lump in my throat. He's so . . . serious and intent, so wrapped up in what he's saying, that you forget he's Will and you completely believe he's the character he's playing. He's lovely to listen to . . . and to watch.

I'm glad he's got the guts to do what he wants.

But I'm scared what will happen when Dad finds out.

I thought things were back to normal with Gran and she'd got over her night-time excursions and the other thing – you know, the enuresis. That means involuntary urination (and that means wetting yourself). I found it by accident last week as part of my latest plan to learn a new word every day. I open the dictionary randomly and stab it with a pencil with my eyes closed.

Today's word was sitophobia – a morbid aversion to food. Gran definitely doesn't suffer from that; she can't stop eating. I earwigged a conversation between Mum and Granddad that made me laugh till I realised it wasn't as funny as it sounded. It took place when Mum and I called in at Gran's one Sunday after our run.

I'd gone into the front room first to rifle through Dad's stuff while they made a cup of tea. Gran's even kept his old school reports in the bottom drawer of the sideboard.

I flicked through his Third Year report. (Year 9 to you.) Hmm. Not everyone thought the sun shone out of Dad's backside in those days. It was like reading my own report. Except for sport he was pretty useless at school. He was brilliant at rugby though.

'Tremendous talent. The youngest pupil ever to represent the school, Robert Ellis has the potential one day to represent his country,' said the neat black handwriting of Mr D. Dawkins, Sports Master. What an accolade!

He didn't though, did he? Represent his country. Not long after Gran proudly handed over that silver medal to him when he made County level, he got his leg smashed up and that was it – the end of all those dreams. Poor Dad, he must have been gutted. I wonder, not for the first time, how it happened. He never talks about it.

I opened the cabinet and took out the medal. This would be Will's one day. I held it up to the light and saw that it was covered in a layer of dust. Unbelievable. I thought Gran made a point of polishing all Dad's trophies every week, but it looked as if it hadn't been touched for months. I breathed on it and rubbed it with the hem of my T-shirt till it gleamed then put it back carefully in pride of place in the cabinet.

Mum and Granddad were in the lounge drinking tea. Gran was fast asleep on the sofa, snoring loudly and they were so deep in conversation by the fire they didn't notice when I slipped in and sat beside Gran.

'When you rang I'd just put the dinner on the table.'

'She didn't make it then?'

'No lass, she's not done that for a long while.' Granddad stared gloomily at the fire, then his shoulders shook and he gave a wry chuckle. 'You'll never guess what she did.'

'What?'

'She ate them both. She ate her dinner and then she ate mine.'

'She ate yours? How did she manage that?' Mum stared at him blankly.

'Well, I went to answer the phone when you rang. We had a bit of a chat like, then you said you wanted to speak to her. She'd finished her dinner by then. Well, I stand by her now when she's on the phone; she's a bit heavy-handed with it nowadays, she's yanked it out of the wall before now. When she'd finished she handed it back to me and went back to the table while I carried on talking to you. By the time I'd got back, she was sitting in my place and she'd eaten my dinner as well. She'd scoffed the lot.'

I giggled and they both turned round to look at me as if they didn't know who I was. Granddad wasn't laughing now and Mum was looking stricken. Mum turned back to him.

'Didn't she remember eating her own?'

'She doesn't remember her own name half the time, Tracy, love.'

Suddenly it wasn't funny any more.

'Have *you* eaten?' asked Mum.

'No. I'm all right. I don't have much of an appetite nowadays.'

'You've got to keep your strength up,' said Mum and they both sighed together and stared into the fire. Beside me Gran gave a huge snore and woke herself up. She blinked at me and patted my hand.

'Hello, Spider, love. You're just in time for dinner.'

Not long after that, Mum started talking about respite care.

'What's that when it's at home?' said Dad.

'You know what I mean. She needs to go into residential care . . .'

My head jerked up in shock. I was about to say, 'NO WAY!' but Dad beat me to it.

'Over my dead body! My mother's not going into a home!'

'I don't mean permanently, you idiot. I'm talking about a short break. Like a holiday, to give your father a rest. He's run ragged looking after Alice.'

'Give over, she's all right.'

'She's *not* all right! He's just doing a great job of making it *look* as if she's all right. He's doing everything in that house, washing, shopping, cleaning, cooking, the lot.'

'Well, there you are then. You said it yourself, he's doing a great job. He doesn't mind looking after her. In sickness and in health and all that.'

Mum shook her head. 'It's not fair on him, Bob. She's getting worse by the day. He has to watch her all the time in case she does something daft or goes off on her own. She asks him the same question a hundred times a day. She panics if he's out of her sight for a minute. He can't even go to the toilet in peace without her banging on the door to see where he is!'

Will and I looked at each other uneasily. We didn't know things had got this bad.

'I'm telling you now, if he doesn't get some help soon he's going to have a breakdown.'

'Okay! I get the message!' Dad yelled. 'But she's not going into a home. That's final! She can come here for a while.'

Mum looked dubious. 'You've no idea—'

'Please, Mum!'

'We can look after her!'

Mum looked from Will to me and gave a big sigh. 'All right,' she said and rubbed her forehead, 'we'll give it

154

a go. Just for a bit to give your Granddad a break. I don't know how we're going to manage though.'

So that's how Gran came to be sitting in our lounge staring blankly at the television screen and wondering aloud every two minutes where Granddad was. (He was at home under strict instructions to rest and recuperate.) And that's how I came to be extradited from my room along with the blow-up mattress.

'Never expected to get so much use out of that thing, did we?' said Mum, nodding at the mattress as I lugged it back into Will's room and threw my sleeping bag on top. She was making up my bed for Gran and the good thing was, this time she'd dug out an old waterproof cover from the attic to put under the sheet.

'How long's she going to be here?' I sat on the floor and watched Mum. I suppose I should have helped but she's got her own way of doing things and she's super-fast. 'Till she gets better?'

Mum plumped up the pillows and smoothed the cover over the bed. 'I don't think she *is* going to get better, love.'

My heart missed a beat. 'What's wrong with her, Mum?' I asked quietly.

'I don't know, Charlotte.' Mum sat down heavily on the bed and looked at me sadly. 'I've got my suspicions but I need to get her to a doctor to find out properly. She won't go for Granddad, stubborn old mule that she is.

She knows that something's not right, poor thing.' A tear rolled down her cheek and I put my arm round her.

'I'll help you with her, Mum,' I said, squeezing her tight.

'I know you will, love, you're really good with her.' I felt a warm glow. 'I just don't know if I can leave her while I go to work. Oh well, we'll see.' She pulled a tissue out of her pocket and blew her nose loudly. 'Come on, let's make some room in your wardrobe so she can hang her things up. And we'll clear a drawer or two for her.'

'Mu-um!'

One glance from Mum shut me up. The glow vanished.

'You were the one who wanted to have her here, Charlotte. Now pick up that stuff on the floor or she'll be breaking her neck.'

That *stuff* was my English project. There was nowhere to put it in Will's room. I didn't want to be in with Will any more. I'd got used to my own space.

Will didn't look too pleased about me invading his either. He pretended he didn't mind but he kept moving my things around. Nothing was ever where I left it.

'Where's my geography homework?' I yelled. I'd overslept after a hot night twisted up in my old nylon sleeping bag with Will's feet dangling out of the bed in direct line with my nose. Now I was running late. 'Mum!'

Mum dashed upstairs looking flustered.

'For goodness' sake, Charlotte, haven't I got enough to do without running round after you!'

'I can't find my homework! Will's moved it!'

Mum found my things under my discarded sleeping bag. My maps, painstakingly coloured in last night, peeked from between my dirty trainers and my unwashed sandwich box. I grabbed them. They were creased up and smeared with mud and coleslaw.

'Will!'

'There's no point in blaming him, he's gone. Anyway, you're the messy one. You'll just have to try and be a bit tidier.'

'There's no room!' I picked bits of carrot off Lake Victoria. 'Have you made my sandwiches?'

'No, I haven't had time. I've had to get your gran up and breakfasted and I'll be late if I don't get a move on.'

I stared at her. 'Are you going in to work?'

'Yes, I've no choice. I've got a business to run.'

'But what about Gran?'

'What about her?' Mum looked at me for a minute as if she was spoiling for a fight. 'I'm going to have to leave her on her own. I've left her some soup to heat up for lunch. Try not to be late home tonight, there's a good girl.'

I opened my mouth to protest but she said, 'Look, I've got to go,' and she fished out her purse and pressed some money into my hand. 'Get yourself a school dinner today.'

'It doesn't work like that!' She wasn't listening. She was off down the stairs and through the front door before I could explain you had to book school dinners for the whole week, so I pocketed the money and picked up some crisps and an apple from the kitchen.

'Bye, Gran. See you tonight.'

I popped my head round the door to the lounge. Gran was sitting in her dressing gown staring at the artificial flames of the gas fire. She looked a bit startled to see me but she smiled and waved.

At lunchtime we had our usual game with the lads. Over the last few weeks this had become a regular fixture, weather permitting. We took it in turns to be captains and pick our own teams. Today it was the turn of Dobbin and Freya. Dobbin went first.

'Spider.'

Wow! It was the first time he'd picked me. Not so long ago he'd objected to me playing at all but now I was his first choice! Careful! Blush alert! Automatically I bent my head to hide my face behind my hair then remembered it didn't work since I'd had my hair cut. I felt Janine's eyes on me so I pretended I was having a coughing fit and that's why I'd gone red and she banged me on the back helpfully.

We had a great game. Dobbin and I made an ace team. We kept passing the ball to each other and scoring and we ran rings round the others. As the bell went the crowd that had gathered to watch burst into applause.

'Nice work,' said Dobbin as we came off the field.

'Thanks.' I smiled at him before I could stop myself. (Idiot. Anyone would think you liked him.) I walked on sharpish before my blushes let me down again. There were only so many coughing fits you could have in one day.

'Spider?' I stopped and turned back to stare at him. He was looking a bit red in the face himself, though I suppose it was because he'd been charging up and down the field for twenty minutes. I mean, I was pretty hot and sweaty too.

He stood there for a moment, hands on his hips, chest rising and falling as he got his breath back. I waited. He was studying his trainers with intense interest.

'Yeah?'

'I wanted to ask you something,' he said, talking to his trainers.

'What?' I glanced down at them. They were covered in mud and grass but they didn't warrant that sort of attention. Puzzled, my eyes moved back to his face.

Suddenly he looked up at me. I'd never noticed before but his eyes were clear and blue. My heart started to thud and I could hear it in my ears.

'I was wondering . . .'

'Great teamwork!' Mr Brady appeared and patted us both on the back. 'I've been watching you two. You've come a long way, both of you. Good to see you've sorted out your differences. Hurry up, Dobson, you'll be late for your lessons. Spider, I want a word with you.'

Dobbin mumbled something and moved off. I watched him go, hardly taking in a word of what Brady was going on about. A message for Mum about a course that was on or something.

Why did he have to come along then?

In geography that afternoon I got told off for my stained and crumpled maps, even though I tried to explain to Mr Evans how it had happened. He wouldn't listen, you could tell he thought I was making it up, and I nearly got a detention for arguing. Teachers!

Mind you, Miss was well impressed with our English project.

'That's coming along nicely, girls. You were wise to choose rugby. You're obviously experts on the game.'

'Spider is, Miss. Her granddad played in the Olympics.'

'Great–great-granddad,' I corrected automatically.

'Did he?' Miss Brown's eyes opened wide. 'That's

amazing! Can you write up an account of it for me for the Open Night display, Charlotte?'

I nodded, proud as punch.

'I'll ask my gran, Miss. She knows all about it.'

I was so keen to do it, I decided to go straight home after school and talk to Gran. I'd do it properly, like a real interview and take notes. Gran would love it. I couldn't wait.

Only when I got home, it didn't work out like that. Because when I put my key in the lock, the first thing I noticed was the smell of burning.

I pushed open the kitchen door and immediately the fire alarm started shrieking in the hall. A saucepan stood on the hob, black and smoking. Inside were the charred remains of what was once Mum's home-made leek and potato soup. I grabbed the handle to yank it into the sink, yelping in pain as a fierce heat burnt into my hand. I turned the tap on to blast cold water over my stinging palm.

'Gran!'

A small figure appeared in the doorway. She was still wearing her dressing gown and slippers, for goodness' sake. What had she been doing all day? She peered at me anxiously.

'Spider? Is that you? What's going on?'

'I've burnt my hand on the saucepan. It's boiled dry on the cooker.'

'Silly girl,' she said, picking up my hand and inspecting my red palm. Small white blisters were already forming. 'You should be more careful. You could have burnt the house down. Let's put some butter on it.'

'No!' I snatched my hand away. 'Screw that noise!' I waved a tea-towel under the smoke alarm and it stopped its high-pitched wailing at last. '*You* left it on, Gran! You forgot the soup.'

'Oh dear.' She looked upset. 'Did I really?' She shuffled out of the kitchen into the hall. I slammed the door shut behind her and stuck my hand under the tap again. Butter! My hand would fry!

The next minute the door opened and the smoke alarm started screeching again. I looked up to see Gran. This time she was wearing her coat over her dressing gown, her bare legs and pink slippers peeping from under it.

'I'd better get off home now, Spider,' she said. 'Your granddad will be waiting for his dinner.'

It was chaos! It was mental! It was funny if it wasn't so awful.

Gran got really stroppy with me because I wouldn't let her go waltzing off to the bus stop in her slippers and nightie. She even pushed me at one point to get out of her way and I banged my shoulder on the wall and then she looked a bit sorry but she was still determined to get out of that door.

In the middle of it all the phone rang and I snatched it up hoping it was Mum but a voice said 'Spider?' and I said 'Yes?' not recognising it at first and then it said, 'It's Wayne. Wayne Dobson' and Gran began shouting and beating on the glass-panelled front door with her fists and I yelled, 'Not now!' and slammed the phone down and I shouted at Gran, 'Stop that right now!' and her legs buckled under her and she sat down on the doormat and started to cry. It was horrible.

I rang Mum at the salon and she could hear Gran crying in this high-pitched keening sound so she got a lift home and rescued us. I was never so pleased to see Mum in my life.

'I didn't know what to do,' I hissed as Mum edged her way through the front door past Gran's hunched body. At least she'd stopped wailing by now. 'She says she's got to go home to make Granddad's dinner. She's already nearly set the house on fire.'

Mum was brilliant. She helped her up and sat her down at the kitchen table and opened the windows wide to let the burning smell out. Then she pulled up a chair next to her while I stood with my back against the door, arms folded, like a jailer.

'Now what's all this about?' Mum asked quietly.

'I can't waste any more time sitting round here,' said Gran. 'Joe wants his dinner.'

'I've told her she's staying with us! Why's she being so stupid?'

Gran glared at me. 'I've been here all day and now *she* won't let me go.'

She looked as if she hated me. I felt like crying.

You know what my lovely mum did? She stood up and gave me a hug.

'She doesn't mean it,' she said to me quietly. I nodded, unable to speak. My throat hurt with unshed tears. She picked up the kettle.

'That's all right, Alice, I'll give you a lift myself. Let's just have a cup of tea first. I've been at work all day, remember?'

By the time Will and Dad came home Gran had calmed down. Mum had even persuaded her to go and get dressed. While Gran was upstairs, she filled Dad in on what had happened.

'You shouldn't have left her on her own all day,' he said.

'What else can I do? I've got a job to go to, same as you. I don't see you offering to take time off to look after her.'

I was about to say I'd stay home from school to care for Gran when I realised I didn't want to. I didn't want to be with Gran, not the way she was now. I'd rather be at school.

'I'm going to have to take her to the doctor's tomorrow, that's for sure,' said Mum. 'She's getting worse.' She glanced at the clock.'What's she doing up there all this time? Run upstairs, Charlotte, and see if she's dressed.'

'Do I have to?'

Dad looked as if he was going to give me a mouthful but Mum laid her hand on his arm.

'Yes please, there's a good girl.'

My bedroom was in darkness. I put my head around

165

the door. I could see a mound in the bed and hear soft snoring.

'She's gone to bed,' I said. 'She's fast asleep.'

Mum looked at Dad and shook her head. 'We won't disturb her. I'll get the tea on and we'll have it in peace.'

Dad and I went into the lounge to watch the news while Mum busied herself in the kitchen. I wasn't really following world events, I had too much going on in my own life, but it gave me space to think under the cover of the newsreader's droning voice. I had a lot to think about, didn't I?

Like, why had Dobbin rung me?

Maybe it wasn't him. Maybe it was someone messing about.

It had sounded like him though.

'Charlie? Do you think your mother's making a fuss about Gran? Is she really that bad?' Dad's voice broke into my thoughts as they whirled around in my head.

'She's worse. She can't be left on her own any more, she's a liability.'

Dad was quiet for a bit. Then he said, 'She's probably just confused, staying here. We'll take her to the doctor's tomorrow and get her sorted.'

'She nearly burnt the house down today, Dad.'

'You're getting as bad as your mum, all doom and gloom.' He rubbed his hand through his hair, the way he always does when he's worried. 'She'll be all right when she's back in her own house.'

Yeah, right. Who was he trying to convince?

A car pulled up outside. Dad stood up to have a look through the curtains and swore under his breath. 'What's he doing here again? He's never off the flaming doorstep.'

I craned to have a look. It was Phil Brady.

'Flipping heck!' I clapped my hand to my mouth. 'It's my maths lesson. I forgot all about it, what with Gran and all that.'

'We haven't even had our tea yet,' muttered Dad, sitting back down with a black look on his face. I let Phil in and we went into the kitchen. Mum looked pleased to see him anyway. He pulled our maths book and a file from his briefcase and started burbling to her about this course he'd been going on about earlier. I hadn't had a chance to pass on his message to Mum, not that I'd been listening anyway.

No one seemed to be in a rush to get on to maths coaching that's for sure.

'Make us a cup of coffee, Charlotte, while I have a quick look at this lot,' said Mum. Soon they were busy, heads down and engrossed, pouring over the stuff in the file. It was from the RFU about setting up women's teams.

Then Dad walked into the kitchen, taking in at a

glance Mum and Phil at the table together, coffee cups in front of them. He frowned. Mum looked up at him and smiled, at the same time deftly closing the file.

'Look who's here!' said Mum, pointing at Phil. 'I'd completely forgotten it was Thursday, what with everything.'

'Hello, Bob. How's your mother?'

'She's all right.' Dad's voice was curt. He pulled out a chair and sat down, his back turned to Phil. Phil studied him for a second then turned to me.

'Ready for your maths lesson, Spider?'

'I wouldn't mind having my tea first if you don't mind,' said Dad, scowling. 'I have been at work all day.'

Mum stared at Dad. Phil stood up and swept the file and the maths book back into his briefcase.

'Of course, sorry, mate. Look, we'll leave it for tonight, Spider.'

Mum looked upset. 'But you've come all this way . . . let me pay you . . .'

'Don't be daft,' said Phil, 'I can see you've got your hands full. See you at school tomorrow, Spider. Bye, Bob.'

Dad grunted. Mum saw him out and I could hear her talking to him in a low voice at the front door. After a while she came back in and stood in front of Dad, her hands on her hips.

'Do you mind telling me what all that was about?'

Dad glared back at her. 'Do *you* mind if we eat first?'

Mum glowered at him for a moment, then she opened the door and yelled, 'Will! Tea's ready!'

Will came in, looked at our faces and sidled into his seat. Mum grabbed a tea-towel and bent down and took plates out of the oven, banging them down in front of us. It was pizza and chips, dry and burnt. I picked up my knife and fork and started eating.

'What's this?' asked Dad. I chewed and chewed then tried to swallow but the pizza lodged in my throat. It wouldn't go down no matter how hard I tried. I could feel myself gagging.

'What's it look like?' snapped Mum.

'Bloody awful to someone who's been grafting all day.'

'*I've* been grafting all day too!' Mum banged the oven tray into the sink. '*And* I've been looking after *your* mother since I came home.'

'Doesn't look like that to me,' said Dad. 'Looks to me like you've been busy enjoying yourself.'

Mum turned around. 'What did you say?'

The room went dangerously quiet. Will slid further down in his chair. I concentrated hard on trying to swallow which had suddenly become the hardest thing in the world to do. I thought it was supposed to be a reflex action. Like breathing. Only now I was holding my breath too.

'Where's Joe?'

No one had noticed Gran standing in the doorway. She was still wearing her coat over her dressing gown, she must have been to bed in it for goodness' sake, and her eyes were screwed up against the light. She rubbed them and peered round anxiously. 'Where's Joe gone?' she repeated.

Mum went to her side and led her to the table. 'Just in time for tea, Alice,' she said. 'What would you like?'

'Just a bit of toast, Tracy, love,' said Gran. 'I don't want to be any trouble.'

She sat down next to Dad and patted his hand. 'Had a nice day, Bob?' she said.

Dad looked as if he was going to choke. He stood up abruptly and shovelled his food in the bin. 'I'm going out for a drink.'

'Bob, wait!' said Mum, but the front door slammed behind him. She sat down at the table next to me, looking stunned.

Will bit his lip, struggling not to cry. I gave up trying to eat and put my fork down. Gran looked at us all, one by one, her eyes moving from one face to the next, then she opened her mouth to speak. Please, Gran, don't ask where Granddad is, I prayed silently. Not again.

'Well!' she said, her eyebrows arched. 'Who rattled his cage?'

There was silence and Mum put her head in her hands. Her shoulders started to shake and she snorted. Will looked at me in alarm.

'Don't cry,' I said, putting my hand on her arm. 'He'll be back soon.'

She raised her head and there were tears in her eyes. She let out a whooping sound.

'I know he will, the big lummox, more's the pity! WHO RATTLED HIS CAGE!'

Her words ended in a screech. She was laughing not crying. Then Gran started as well, then Will joined in, then I did; it was so funny you couldn't help it. And soon we were all howling our heads off and when we finally stopped, Gran said, 'You're all mad, the lot of you,' and that started us all off again.

The next day I woke up in agony with a sore throat. Great, I thought, now I've permanently damaged my vocal cords, trying to force pizza down my throat last night and then all that screeching, but Mum had a look and said I had white spots on my tonsils and it looked like I had an infection.

'Come with me to the doctor's when I take Gran,' she said. 'He might give you something for it and she'll come without a fuss because she'll think we're taking you. Brilliant!'

Thanks, Mum. Never mind that I could be dying from some deadly disease like diphtheria or yellow fever or . . . leprosy or something – just as long as I can be useful, then don't you worry about me.

So that's how I ended up in the surgery listening to Dr Keen asking Gran loads of questions. It's a great name for a doctor, isn't it? I mean, you wouldn't want one called Dr Can't-Be-Bothered, would you? He is keen too, very thorough according to Mum, not like the old one who once fell asleep apparently when a friend of Gran's was telling him all about her lumbago. (What is lumbago, I wonder?)

He examined me first, looking down my throat with a torch, and fortunately for Mum it was just tonsillitis. I asked if I could have that nice sweet yellow medicine I used to have when I was a kid and he said no, there was no need, it would clear up on its own, so I thought, hmm, you're a bit too laid back for my liking actually, Dr Keen, but then he said I should stay off school till I felt better and he zoomed up again in my estimation.

Then he turned his attention to Gran and asked her if she minded me being there while he examined her (blooming cheek) but luckily she said, 'No, she's no trouble,' as if I was six. I was glad because I'm nosy by nature, I can't help it, and I wanted to see what was going on. It was a real eye-opener, I can tell you, because then Dr Keen became Dr Super-Diligent.

He started off asking her dead easy stuff like what day of the week it was, what month, what season, what year, etc., but do you know, Gran got them all wrong. I couldn't believe it; she sat there looking as normal as could be, very smart in her best coat with her hair done lovely, Mum made sure of that, but she didn't have a clue.

She answered firmly and clearly and if you didn't know she was wrong, you would have sworn she was right, if you know what I mean, but there was no way it was a Saturday in spring in 1957. I mean, come on, if she'd worked it out, that would have made her a teenager.

Some of the stuff was quite hard; I even had trouble doing it. For instance, she had to count back from one hundred in multiples of seven, like one hundred, ninety-three, eighty-six, seventy-nine . . . you see what I mean? I mean, why would you ever need to do that anyway? But when he asked her to name two main streets in the town she was spot on, because she came back, quick as a flash, with the two roads running round the rugby ground. Mum smiled at me when Dr Keen gave her a point for those.

But then he gave her some instructions which she had to read and carry out and she was hopeless. It was easy stuff like folding paper or closing your eyes but she couldn't manage it. Soon she wasn't scoring at all and you could see she was getting tired and agitated, so Dr Keen abandoned the test and just talked to her gently and she calmed down. Then he said he wanted to talk to Mum on her own so I took Gran back to the waiting room and one of those old ladies who act as volunteers at the surgery gave us a cup of tea and a biscuit. And I looked at the volunteer and I thought, she's loads older than my gran and she can still make a cup of tea without burning the place down, and I felt really sad.

Gran squeezed my hand and whispered, 'Buck up, chuck. It may never happen,' and I wanted to cry. Then the door opened and Mum came out and I saw her face and I knew she was feeling the same.

You see, this is the examination you don't want to pass. You do so by getting most of the answers wrong and this confirms what's wrong with you. My gran passed with flying colours.

'Acute Confusional State.' That's what Gran's got. It's not an exact diagnosis and they've still got to do lots more tests to find out exactly what's causing it, but basically she's suffering from some kind of dementia.

She's losing her mind. She's going mad. And it can only get worse.

I was off school for a week with my sore throat. It spread to my glands and I couldn't swallow and I felt sooo sorry for myself, which was just as well because no one else did. Mum said, 'Poor Charlotte,' but with a gleam in her eye which told me she was really thinking, 'Yippee, you'll be at home to look after Gran now.' And Will turned away from me and slept with his face to the wall so he wouldn't get the dreaded lurgy and have to miss the show, that's how much he cared, while I tossed and turned on the blow-up mattress and felt as if red-hot needles were piercing my throat.

Actually, it's not quite true that no one felt sorry for me. Gran did. She came up trumps, reverting to nursemaid mode, raiding the freezer for ice-cream for my poorly throat and checking up on me every two minutes to see if I was still alive. It was like she had switched on again because she was needed.

Granddad came round to see how I was and he said, 'You need your own bed Spider love' and that afternoon, when I was asleep, he took her home with him on the bus. Mum and Dad were worried when they came home but I croaked, 'He's looking loads better.'

Dad popped round to see them. When he got back he said, 'They're fine. That rest has done him the world of good,' and Mum looked relieved and let it go.

That night she changed my bed, the one that Gran had been sleeping in, and said, 'Now get some sleep', turning off my mobile. I did as I was told, creeping back in gratefully, and slept on and off for the next three days.

When I got up to rejoin the land of the living, Mum said my friends had never stopped ringing.

'Becky's been calling every day,' she said. 'And Janine's rung and Chloe and Freya . . . I never knew you were so popular!'

I smiled. I didn't either. I scrolled through my phone. They'd texted me loads too.

'Oh,' she added carelessly, as if it had slipped her mind. 'Someone called Wayne rang too.'

'Wayne?' I echoed, equally casual. 'What did he want?'

'Your father answered. Bob? What did that Wayne want?'

'I don't know,' said Dad. 'I told him to bugger off!'

'Da-ad!' I hoped he was joking. 'What did he say?'

'Not a lot. He wanted to speak to you. I told him he couldn't, you were in bed. End of story.'

Thanks, Dad.

'What's he doing ringing you anyway?' persisted Dad.

I shrugged, pretending indifference. 'He's just a mate.'

Inside I was bursting. I mean, I didn't know why he'd rung. He wasn't a mate. He was my worst enemy. He hated me. I hated him. It had always been like that.

Not any more.

So why was he ringing me?

Why did boys normally ring girls?

To ask them out.

Don't be stupid.

It was good to be back at school. Everyone said they'd missed me which made me feel good. Loads had happened in the space of a week.

Chloe and Freya had been round to Janine's for a sleepover and they said her house was haunted (I wish I'd been there); Chloe had dumped Craig and transferred her affections to Gavin; Mr Brady had torn Bev off a strip at training on Friday night and she'd burst into tears and said she was never coming back and he'd had to take her home in his car; Dale the Fail had had another go at Dobbin and Dobbin had told him where to go in no uncertain terms and now he was on his final warning and threatened with suspension if he stepped out of line again. (Dobbin I mean, not Dale, unfortunately.)

But I still didn't know why Dobbin had rung. At breaktime and lunchtime he was nowhere to be seen and I wondered if he was avoiding me.

We had maths last and I could have strangled Dale. He started us on a new topic, Probability, outlining what we were going to do on the board in about six seconds flat. Then he wiped it off and fired questions round the class to see how much we'd taken in. He didn't want to make it easy for us, he wanted to make it as difficult as possible because he thought it made him look big. If he only knew!

Anyway, it was okay for me, I'd gone over this already with Phil so I could keep up, but Dobbin was lost. He just sat there in silence while Dale tried to wind him up with original and witty (not) comments like, 'Cat got your tongue?' and 'Are we keeping you awake, Dobson?' No one laughed because we could all see what he was up to, trying to provoke him so he'd get suspended.

So when he got no reaction the Maths Monster started to get more personal, saying stupid things like, 'Never mind, I'm sure there's something we can find that you are good at. Let me see. Knitting? Sewing? Bit of cookery?' I hate the way he does that, says 'WE' so that you become part of the taunting, whether you like it or not. It's not fair; there's a big anti-bullying campaign going on in our school yet creeps like Dale get away with it because they're teachers. And I could see that he was pushing, pushing, pushing Dobbin till he was on the point of exploding.

So all of a sudden I thrust my hand in the air and, without waiting to be asked I said, 'He's brilliant at rugby, Sir!' and everyone clued in and they all stuck their hands up and shouted out things Dobbin was good at like, 'He's ace at computer games!' and 'He's good at making us laugh!' and stuff like that then Craig yelled, 'He does a mean impression of you, Sir!' and everyone roared. Then Dale got shirty and threatened us all with detention and we simmered down but he knew he'd lost it.

Even so, as we trooped out I could see that Dobbin was still taut as a string on a bow because he said, 'I hate ******* maths,' and he looked really miserable.

'It's not maths you hate, it's Dale,' I said, trying to cheer him up, but he shook his head.

'It's all right for you, you can do it now. It takes me ages to get my head round what we're doing and just as I'm starting to get the hang of it we move on to a new topic. Now we've started on Probability I'm lost again.'

That was some admission from Dobbin. If he couldn't do something, he'd always made out he didn't want to. I looked up at him as he slouched along beside me, shoulders slumped and hands in his pockets, looking the picture of misery. Even though he was about ten metres taller than Dale, the dwarf could still make him feel small. I felt a sharp pang of sympathy.

'I can give you a hand with Probability if you like. Mr Br . . . someone showed me how to do it and it's dead easy when you know how.'

He stopped and stared at me in surprise and I braced myself for a sharp retort like, 'Who do you think you are, Brain of Britain?' or something like that but instead he said, 'Do you mean it?' and I said, 'Yeah, of course I do,' and he smiled and said 'Thanks!' and we stood there grinning at each other and I felt all warm inside.

And I wondered why I'd spent all those years hating Dobbin.

He slung his bag on the ground and leant against the wall.

'We could get together one day next week,' he suggested. 'It's half term.'

Oh my goodness. This was it. A date!

'If you like,' I said, like I didn't care.

'Come round to mine?'

'Whatever.'

'That's really good of you, Spider.'

'S'all right.'

'Okay then,' he grinned, picking up his bag. 'See you next week.'

'Right.'

Since when had I been lost for words? He must have thought I'd been struck dumb or something. It was like the part of my brain controlling my speech had been switched off and the part of my brain that noticed things had taken over.

Things like, when did your zits disappear?

Things like, you've got such a great smile.

Things like, when did you get to be so fit?

He slung his bag over his shoulder and turned to walk away. My brain shifted back into verbal gear. Sort of.

'When do you want me? To do it? Maths, I mean,' I stumbled, feeling my inner glow move up to my cheeks and combust into a raging fire.

'When it's convenient for you,' he said, looking at me curiously. 'Are you all right?'

'Feverish,' I said, fanning myself furiously with my maths book. 'Left over from my tonsillitis. I'll come round Thursday.'

What a plonker! I wasn't even sure where he lived.

'Riverside Flats,' he said, reading my mind. 'Second floor, number sixteen. See you.'

Morning? Afternoon? Too late, he'd gone.

Becky rang me on Saturday to see if I wanted to go to town but I was trying to save up for Christmas so I said no. The Tinners were playing away and Will was out and in the end I stayed in on my own.

So I dug out the work I'd done with Phil and went over it, making sure I could explain it to Dobbin clearly and simply. Because I'd realised that was why Dale was such a crap teacher, he made Maths more complicated than it really was. I was actually looking forward to going round to Dobbin's and working mathematical wizardry on him like Phil had done on me.

After that there was nothing to do. I mooched around the house, wandering in and out of rooms, and spent a while rummaging through Mum's stuff. She was quite trendy for an oldie. Now she'd gone down a size or two I could nearly fit into some of her clothes. There was nothing there I'd want to be seen in though.

I decided to have a pampering afternoon. Becky would be proud of me. I had a long hot bath full to the brim with foaming bath essence and shampooed and conditioned my hair. I debated straightening it but in the end I blow-dried it in front of Mum's dressing-table mirror, going for the tousled look. It looked good. I decided I would wear it like this when I went round to Dobbin's.

Then I got carried away. I spotted Mum's impressive tweezers, the ones she uses in the salon, and thought it was time I tidied up my eyebrows. I started by plucking a few stray hairs from underneath like I'd seen Mum do.

I did the right one first and that was fine but then I went a bit mad with the left. The trouble is, you're up so close to the mirror when you're doing it and your skin is all stretched out and you're concentrating, and . . . Help! When I sat back to admire my handiwork I saw that my left eyebrow was now arching provocatively about two centimetres above the other.

I looked like Dale the Fail about to launch into sarcastic mode.

There was nothing for it but to match the right with the left.

I gritted my teeth and got to work. It wasn't easy. Mum's tweezers were extra sharp and soon the skin beneath my brows was covered in hundreds of tiny red pimples which made it really difficult to see if they were matching. I was concentrating so hard when my phone rang it made me jump and I pulled out more than I intended.

It was Becky. In excitable mode.

'Spider! You'll never guess what I'm going to do . . . !'

I had a gap in my right eyebrow.

'I just want to see if it's okay with you first . . .'

I looked like I'd had a piercing removed.

'I won't do it if you don't want me to . . .'

Plus I looked permanently surprised.

'Only I'm sure you won't be bothered . . .'

Everyone would laugh. It was all Becky's fault.

'Do what you want.'

There was a pause. Then Becky's voice came on, nonplussed.

'But I haven't told you yet.'

I looked like a clown with two eyebrows drawn on in semi-circles. One with a gap in it. Panic set in.

'Becky, I don't care what you do. Leave me alone!'

I stabbed my phone off and threw it out of the window. I could hear it ringing again somewhere in the flowerbeds but I was otherwise engaged, sobbing my head off.

Mum tried her best when she came home but even she couldn't stick them back on. But she did take a bit more off the ends which meant they didn't bend quite so alarmingly and she filled in the gap with eyebrow pencil, saying, 'You'll have to remember to do this till it grows back.'

'It will grow back, won't it?' I hiccuped, staring at myself in the mirror.

'Of course it will,' she said snapping her beauty bag shut. 'Now lay off my stuff in future.' She studied me in the mirror. 'Your hair looks nice by the way. And no one will notice you've overdone the plucking.'

On Monday, ('Oh my goodness, Spider, what have you done to your eyebrows?') we trained on the school field because it was half term and Phil had something he wanted to do on Friday. I was ready to apologise to Becky for snapping at her, having got used to the bald look by now, but she turned up late.

Phil was coaching us on multi-directional moves, zigzagging, jumping up, skipping backwards, running sideways, all that sort of stuff. It was fast and full on and you had to concentrate hard and there was no time to say anything. When we finished I went up to her and she looked a bit wary, probably afraid I was going to bite her head off again, but before I could say sorry, Chloe said, 'Look who's here,' and I turned to see Dobbin on his own, watching us.

He raised his hand and waved and Becky and I waved back.

He'd come to meet me.

'What's he hanging about for?' said Chloe.

'Trying to pick up some tips,' said Janine. We all groaned because she'd just come in for some praise from Phil for coming on so well.

'He fancies you, Spider, didn't you know?' said Freya.

I felt a surge of happiness but, unable to break the habit of a lifetime, pretended to shiver. 'Give me a break.'

Becky swung her bag on her shoulder and pulled her ponytail tighter. 'Actually,' she said, 'he's waiting for me.'

We gaped as she waltzed up to him and they stood

talking, Becky smiling up at him and tossing her hair.

'What's she like? She's flirting with him! She creases me up,' giggled Chloe and I joined in, wondering what Becky was up to.

The smile slid from my lips as she slipped her arm through his, waved at us with a cheeky grin and strolled off with him out of the school gates. Freya and Chloe burst out laughing.

'You should see your face!' cried Freya.

'She's winding me up!' I appealed. 'Tell me she's not serious.'

'She looked pretty serious to me,' said Freya and went off into fits of giggles again and I pretended I found it pretty hilarious too.

But inside I was seething. How long had this been going on? And why had they kept me in the dark?

Becky was supposed to be my best friend!

And Dobbin. I thought he was going to ask *me* out!

I bet they were having a huge laugh at my expense.

I felt sooo stupid.

I pulled on my trackie top and walked home on my own, steaming.

By the time I got home Becky was texting me but I ignored her. Later on that night she rang me on the landline and Mum called me down so I had to speak to her.

'Why didn't you answer my calls?' she said.

'My phone was switched off.'

'Why?'

'Got stuff to do. Anyway, I thought you were busy.'

There was a pause. 'Spider?'

'What?'

'I'm sorry I didn't tell you about . . .'

'What?'

'You know.'

'No I don't know. I don't know what's going on at all.' Silence. 'Are you going out with Dobbin?'

Another pause. 'Yes.'

'You're kidding!'

'No I'm not.' Her tone became a bit frosty. 'And his name's Wayne, by the way.'

I took time to digest this. Then I said, 'Why didn't you tell me?'

'I tried to. On Saturday. But you slammed the phone down on me.'

Of course I did. Because you made me amputate half my eyebrow, that's why. But that didn't make any difference. She'd still pinched what should've been my first date from under my nose.

'Spider? Speak to me.' She sounded as if she was going to cry. 'I knew you'd react like this.'

'Why?' I said frostily.

'You said he was a geek, a freak and a loser, remember?'

Did I? Suddenly I realised that everyone thought I couldn't stand Dobbin. Including Becky.

So I might feel stupid but at least I didn't have to look it.

I took a deep breath. Then I said, 'He *is* all those things. I know him. I know what he's like.'

There was a huge silence then I asked, 'How long have you and the loser been going out anyway?'

'Only since Saturday.' Becky ignored the insult, eager to make amends. 'I met him in town and we got talking and before I knew it he asked me out. Actually, that's not quite true, I asked him out and he said yes.'

I bet he did, I thought grimly.

'I wanted to check with you first but you wouldn't speak to me . . .' Her voice trailed away. 'He's nice, Spider. When you get to know him, he's really nice.'

I know he is . . . I know that now . . . But she'd got in first and now they were a couple.

I felt really left out.

But I was NEVER, EVER going to let them know how I felt.

'What? Nice as in stuffing spiders down your neck? Or in calling you names and getting you into trouble at every opportunity? He doesn't give a stuff about anyone but himself, Becks. I grew up with the guy, remember?'

'That's the trouble. I mean, he was only a kid then.

He's a different person now. He's thoughtful . . . and sensitive . . .'

'Oh really? Like a snake in the grass is thoughtful and sensitive! Like a crocodile on a river bank is thoughtful and sensitive. Like a . . . maggot in a sheep's bum is thoughtful and sensitive!'

The phone went dead.

Okay, I'd got carried away. Perhaps the maggot image was a bit strong; they're horrible things, they eat the poor sheep alive. I saw it on the telly.

Mind you, I can't imagine anyone eating Becky alive.

The phone rang and I grabbed it.

'People change, Spider.' Becky's voice was huffy.

I snorted. 'Yeah, right.'

'He's matured. Perhaps you should try it. And, by the way, you've overdone the eyebrow shaping!'

This time *I* slammed the phone down. The cheek of it! Who was *she* to call me immature? Little Miss Girly, Little Miss Glam, Little Miss Cutesy, Little Miss Wannabee . . . URRGH! Words failed me. I might be immature but at least I didn't dump my best mate as soon as a bloke looked at me.

But when I calmed down I felt really miserable.

They weren't going to want me around any more, that's for sure.

'She hasn't dumped you. Anyway, no bloke *would* look at you.' I threw a pillow at Will. I was lying on his bed the next day, bending his ear about Becky and Dobbin, but he wasn't being very helpful. He was far too wrapped up in becoming word-perfect for *A Plague on Your Town*. And being as Becky was his leading lady, she could do no wrong in his eyes. As if he could read my mind he said, 'Lucky Dobbin. I wouldn't mind going out with Becky, she's gorgeous.'

'You're too young.' I felt a sharp pang of jealousy, like a real pain. I'd always been the special person in Will's life before Becky had come on the scene. Now they thought the sun shone out of each other. Maybe she'd only befriended me because I was Will's sister.

I sat up and stared in his mirror. We certainly looked alike, Will and me. Everyone thought he was gorgeous but did that make me nice-looking? I studied my face.

Brown eyes with flecks of green and longish eyelashes; fairish-brown hair, feathered by Mum into trendy style; splodgy little nose with a smattering of freckles; small scar on chin where a hockey ball had jumped off someone's stick.

Did my chin jut out too much? Did my left ear stick out further than my right? Would anyone call *me* gorgeous? Unlikely, with those Coco the Clown eyebrows.

'D'you think Becky's better-looking than me?'

Will sighed and put down his script and came and sat next to me on the bed, cocking his head on one side and contemplating me in the mirror. I wished I hadn't asked.

'I dunno,' he said at last. 'You're my sister, I can't tell. You're different from Becky, but you're all right. I feel happy when I look at you.'

Aah, thanks Will. I don't think that's the answer I was looking for, but it made me feel good anyway. 'Give us your script, I'll test you,' I said, feeling generous, and his face lit up.

It was half term and there was nothing to do. I wasn't even going to have my maths lesson this week from Phil and it shows how sad my life had become that I was disappointed. We were supposed to be looking after Gran while Granddad had a tidy up at home but it wasn't exactly difficult. Since she'd been on the tablets the doctor had given her she'd quietened down and seemed to nap most of the day. She'd even stopped asking where Granddad was when he wasn't around.

It was a grey, cold day outside but in Will's bedroom it was snug and warm. We went straight through the text, Will taking his part and me playing Becky's role, and we got really wrapped up in it. I could see the attraction.

Will was standing on his bed singing his solo, giving it everything he'd got, and I was sitting cross-legged on the floor, swaying in time to the song, when the door suddenly opened. It was Dad. Will stopped in mid-note.

'What's going on?' Dad asked, his eyes scanning the room and coming back to rest on Will. 'Why's your gran on her own downstairs?'

'We're just messing about,' I said hurriedly. 'Gran's all right.'

'No she's not, she's down there on her own wondering where everyone is. She's wondering where *she* is, in fact. I thought you two would do a better job of looking after her than this.' He glared at Will. 'And what's all that wailing about?'

'Nothing.' Will got off the bed. His face had that closed-in look again. I kicked the script carefully under the bed away from Dad's prying eyes.

'Is Mum home?' I asked, scrambling to my feet. I didn't want Dad to start on Will. He never used to be like this;

at one time Will could do no wrong.

'Not yet. God knows where she's got to.' Dad ran his hand through his hair and turned away, then he hesitated. 'I'd better run your gran home in the van. Coming?'

Will looked at me and pulled a face. Lucky for him, Dad didn't see him as he was already halfway down the stairs. I grabbed him by the hand.

'Come on, it won't take long and then you can get back to your precious play.'

Gran sat in the front seat and asked where we were going. 'Home,' said Dad firmly, but two minutes later she asked again. Will and I started giggling and when she asked a third time Dad said, 'Alton Towers.' Will laughed out loud but I saw Gran's face and she looked really confused so I butted in with, 'We'll be home in a minute, Gran,' and she sat back and relaxed. Dad looked at me sheepishly in the mirror.

'Well done, Charlie,' he said. Poor Dad, he looked tired. I could see a small bald spot at the back of his head and I pointed it out to Will and he started giggling again and then I felt mean. Dad would hate it if he knew.

Gran's hair looked messy too. I suppose I should have made sure she put a comb through it before we left the house. Life is weird. It wasn't so long ago she was telling me to take more pride in myself and now she couldn't look after herself properly. And she certainly didn't notice when I put on something new or wore a bit of make-up.

Because I do now, sometimes. That's Becky's influence. Becky. I hadn't heard from her since the row. Flipping heck. I stared gloomily out of the window pondering on the unfairness of life.

'The doctor's coming round to do an assessment on your mother tomorrow, Bob,' said Granddad as he helped Gran out of the car. 'Can you be here?'

'I'm not sure,' said Dad. Granddad looked worried and Dad added quickly. 'Aye, one of us'll be there, either me or Tracy.'

When we got home, Mum was having a shower.

'Where have you been?' asked Dad grumpily as she came out wrapped in a towel.

'I went for a run after work. No law against that is there?'

'You're keep-fit mad all of a sudden,' grumbled Dad. Mum looked a bit uneasy. I jumped in with, 'Gran's seeing the doctor tomorrow. He's going to her house to assess her. Granddad wants you or Dad to be there.'

'I can't,' said Dad immediately. 'I'm behind with the job already. You'll have to go, Trace.'

'You must be joking! I'm booked solid all day!'

'Well, you'll just have to unbook then,' snapped Dad. 'Now where's my tea?'

Before she stormed upstairs and slammed the bedroom door, Mum told him very clearly and precisely where he could find it though personally I would say it was anatomically impossible for it to be there.

In the morning they'd both calmed down but they still hadn't resolved who was going to take time off work.

'Time's money, Trace.'

Mum chewed at the skin around her thumbnail, a sure sign she was worried. 'Someone needs to be there.'

'I'll do it. I'll go round, Mum. I'm off school anyway.'

Mum looked grateful. 'Thanks, Charlotte. Take Will with you.'

Will wrinkled his nose and said nothing. Actually, it wasn't like me to be so obliging. But I had nothing else to do that Thursday.

I mean Dobbin wouldn't want me to coach him in maths now, would he?

Not now he had Becky to show him a thing or two.

Dr Keen's getting to know me; we've seen a lot of each other recently. We're almost on first-name terms. (His name's Malcolm by the way.)

'Hello again,' he said when I answered the door to him. 'No school?'

What is it with adults? I wouldn't say to him 'No work, Malcolm?' if I saw him in Tesco's.

'Half term,' I said, opening the door wide. 'Come on in.'

'You in charge then?' he said, wiping his feet. I didn't deign to answer. Will certainly wasn't, that's for sure. He'd scooted off to rehearsal as soon as Mum and Dad had left for work. I noticed immediately how the doctor took everything in with a sweeping glance around the room and I was pleased that it was neat and tidy. Under Mum's instructions I'd made sure the breakfast things were washed up and everything was in its place before the doctor came. And, of course, I made sure Gran was presentable.

Her face lit up when she saw him. 'How about a cup of tea?' she asked.

'I'll make it.'

'No.' Dr Keen put his hand on my arm. 'Let your gran do it. Milk, no sugar please.'

I sat down, clocking what he was up to. Gran bustled off to the kitchen and the doctor took out a notebook and pen.

'So how's she been?' he asked 'Less anxious now?'

'Those tablets seem to be doing the trick,' said Granddad.

'Good. Can she wash herself, bath, manage the toilet?'

Come on, Malcolm! What sort of question is that? I picked up a newspaper and became intensely interested in yesterday's news while Granddad leant forward and whispered in his ear.

'Hmm.' Doctor Keen scribbled in his notebook. 'What about sleeping?'

'Up and down all night long. The tablets don't seem to work at night.'

'And you? Are you managing to get some sleep?'

Granddad shrugged. 'You know how it is . . .'

Doctor Keen studied him for a while then he said, 'Let's check you out while we're here' and took out his stethoscope and listened to Gramps' heart.

At that moment Gran came in, carrying a tray, 'His chest playing him up again?' she asked conversationally but she didn't look a bit concerned. I took the tray from her and put it down on the table. It seemed okay. There were only three cups (not enough but I didn't want one anyway), no saucers, but what the heck. There was milk in a jug and she'd even put some of the biscuits I'd brought over this morning on a plate. Well done, Gran. I smiled at her, pleased that she'd managed on her own.

'Shall I pour the tea?'

'Yes please, love. Be careful, it's hot.'

Only it wasn't. It was stone cold. I could tell as soon as I started pouring it; there was no steam or heat and the tea came out like water. She'd forgotten to boil the kettle. She offered the biscuits around and I took the teapot out to the kitchen, emptied it, boiled the kettle and made a fresh pot. She never even noticed. Dr Keen did though. He wrote it down in his notebook.

'Keeping well, Alice?' he asked.

'You know me, Doctor. Strong as an ox. I'm never ill.'

It was true. She never seemed to catch cold or be off colour. Gran went on, warming to an audience. 'We both keep well, don't we, Joe? Do you know, Doctor, neither of us have had a day's illness in our lives.'

I glanced at Gramps, all grey and old and washed out,

and wondered what was going on in her head. She'd just mentioned his bad chest but she'd forgotten it already. Did she think this was just a courtesy call? Did she think this is what doctors spent their time doing, coming round for a cup of tea?

Obviously. Gran, in her element with someone new to talk to, chatted away happily about her favourite topic, the Tinners.

'My son plays for them, you know,' she said. 'Robert Ellis. He plays on the wing.' Gramps and I looked at each other and Gramps shook his head slightly. Say nothing. 'Do you follow them, Doctor?'

'When I can,' he said. 'Robert Ellis? Doesn't ring a bell.'

After he'd gone I made another cup of tea and a sandwich for us all and then I decided to get a move on. Because I'd been thinking.

Maybe Dobbin *was* expecting me to turn up after all. I mean, there was no reason why he shouldn't, he had no idea I thought he was going to ask me out.

And he didn't know all the stuff I'd said about him either, all the stupid, childish names I'd called him.

Unless Becky had told him.

No she wouldn't. He was probably waiting for me now, wondering where I was.

How could I find out? I didn't know his mobile

number. I didn't even know his landline. And I certainly wasn't going to ask Becky.

Come on, Spider, get a grip. They didn't invent telephone directories for nothing.

I pored through Gran's but, though there were loads of Dobsons, there were none living at Riverside Flats. There was nothing for it but to go round. By now I had convinced myself he would be waiting for me, maths book open, pen at the ready.

I hoped he was. Because, to tell the truth, I couldn't stand this. I hated falling out with my mates. I'm not one of those girls who thrives on the drama of breaking up and making up with their friends. And it wasn't just my best mate I was missing.

I wanted to be mates with Dobbin as well. If that's all I could be. I mean, if those two were a couple, it didn't mean we couldn't all be friends, did it? Especially as they had no idea about my true feelings.

So in the end I got a bus over to Riverside Flats. It's on a new housing estate on the other side of town, by the river, obviously. It was easy to find. I ran up the stairs to the second floor and walked along the outside corridor to number sixteen.

I rang the bell but there was no reply. Damn, what a waste of time. I could hear shouts and laughter coming from the play park round the corner so I went to the end of the walkway and peered over the balcony. There was a group of mums with buggies, chatting while their toddlers played in the sandpit, some boys doing wheelies on their bikes, and a smattering of kids on the play equipment.

At the far end two older kids were standing on the big swings, soaring up into the air, pushing strongly with their legs, to and fro. They were racing each other, seeing who could go the highest. I could hear them yelling and laughing. The boy was winning but the girl leant back as she kicked upwards, trying hard to catch up, her blonde hair streaming out behind her. It was Becky and Dobbin.

Suddenly Dobbin, showing off, parachuted off the swing. He landed awkwardly, rolling over and over until he came to a halt and lay, spread-eagled and still, on the sand, his face turned up to the grey sky. My heart stopped.

Becky sat down immediately, braking with her feet, then she jumped off the swing and knelt at his side. Below me I could see the women had ceased talking to stare at what was going on. The air seemed still as if the whole world was waiting to see what would happen next.

What did happen was Dobbin suddenly sat upright, seized a handful of sand and stuffed it down Becky's neck. She squealed and was up and after him, grabbing hold of his jacket before he could get away and wrestling him to the ground. She was always ace at tackling. She scooped up handfuls of sand herself and threw it all over him. Their peals of laughter echoed around the park. The women went back to their conversation.

I'm an idiot.

He wasn't waiting for me at all. He'd forgotten all about me, he was having such a good time with Becky.

They were both having a ball. Without me.

I saw the bus coming in the distance and turned away. I could get it if I ran.

I went round to Gran's the next day as well to check the oldies were both all right. I washed up the breakfast things and peeled the potatoes for tea. I did their bit of shopping, mainly bread, milk, fruit and veg, and I even put the Hoover over the lounge and the stair carpet. I didn't go into their bedroom or ask if they wanted their washing doing, mind you. That was too personal. I left that for Mum to do at the weekend.

'She's been as good as gold, our Spider,' said Granddad to Mum who was doing a Sunday roast for us all at their house. Mum smiled at me.

'What about Will? Have you seen much of him?'

'Not so much,' said Granddad. 'I expect he's been busy.'

Too right he has. He's had rehearsals every day at the town hall, I know that for a fact. Because I rang Becky in the end and asked if she wanted to meet up (I was really missing her, if you must know, and I hate being on my own) but she froze me out. Well, what she actually said was, she couldn't, she was rehearsing, and I thought, yeah, yeah, you're really seeing Dobbin, you'd rather spend your time with him. But Will told me it was true, they were practising every day, either in the morning or the afternoon and sometimes all day, so you can see why I didn't mind going round to Gran and Granddad's. It was something to do.

When we were all at the table with Mum plonking plates piled high with roast beef and Yorkshire pudding in front of us, her mobile went off.

'Get that for me,' she said to Will who was nearest to it.

'Mum!' he yelled. 'Phil Brady wants to speak to you!'

Dad glowered and said, 'What the hell does he want now?' but it was Gran's reaction that made us all sit up.

'Phil Brady!' she said. 'That's him!'

We all stared at her. Her face was red with rage.

'That's the bugger! I'll never forget that name as long as I live!'

She struggled to stand up, hemmed in as she was behind the table.

'Here! Give me that phone. I'll tell him what I think of him!'

Mum looked alarmed. She thrust a plate into my hand and said, 'Give this to your dad,' and took the phone off Will and left the room. Gran tried to climb over Will to follow her.

'Sit down, Alice,' said Granddad, trying to pull her back. 'It's over and done with now.'

'Not for my son, it isn't,' Gran shrieked, pushing his hand away. 'He's ruined my son's life!'

I looked at Dad in amazement. He picked up the salt cellar and shook it liberally over his dinner.

'Give over, Mum,' he said. His face was white, but his voice was calm. 'It's in the past.'

'What's he done?' I hadn't realised I'd said these words aloud till Gran's voice spat back at me, beside herself with fury.

'He's broken my Robert's leg, that's what he's done!' Gran's voice cracked and she sat down suddenly. 'Now he can't play rugby any more.'

Tears rolled down her cheeks. She was heartbroken.

It took a moment for me to work it out. Phil Brady was responsible for ruining my dad's rugby career. I looked at Dad and wondered how he could go on spearing carrots, chewing and swallowing, as if nothing had happened. I never knew he was so forgiving. How could he bear to even pass the time of day with him?

'We'll have no dirty play on my team, Wayne Dobson!'

Hypocrite! He'd broken Dad's leg!

My dad was a saint.

And my coach was a sanctimonious, two-faced sinner.

By the time Mum came back in Gran had calmed down and was absorbed in her dinner so no one said 'What did Phil Brady want?' in case it started her off again.

That night when we got home I had a lot of sorting out to do for school. Parents' Evening was on Wednesday and I had to have all my stuff ready for the display on rugby. I knew how important it was to present things properly so I spent hours cutting and sticking and mounting my material on card. At last I was finished and it looked fantastic. I went downstairs to get a drink and say goodnight. Dad was slumped in front of the telly on his own.

'Where's Mum?'

'She's just slipped out to the late night shop to get something for your sandwiches tomorrow.'

'Dad?' I perched on the arm of his chair and draped myself round his neck.

'What?'

'Was Gran right? What she said about Phil Brady?'

Dad shifted. 'Don't take any notice of your gran. It was a long time ago.'

'But was he the person who broke your leg?' I persisted. I needed to know. He sighed.

'It was just a tackle, Charlie. That's rugby. These things happen.'

What a hero! I planted a kiss on his head, just where the hair was thinning, and went into the kitchen to help myself to some milk. The fridge was full of sandwich stuff for the week, cheese, eggs, ham, pâté. What was Mum thinking of? I drank my milk, wiped off my moustache and rinsed the glass under the tap.

'Night, Dad!'

'Night, Charlie. Make sure your brother's light is out.'

I was nearly at the top of the stairs when the front door opened and Mum came in. I was about to call goodnight to her but something stopped me in my tracks. It was the expression on her face. She looked angry and worried at the same time.

And suddenly I knew the real reason she'd been out. It wasn't for sandwich fillings at all. It was something to do with that mysterious phone call from Phil.

I mean, why did he have her mobile number in the first place? Okay, they were running the women's rugby teams together, I'm not stupid, but why was he ringing her on it on a family Sunday afternoon?

And what was so important she couldn't talk to him about it in front of us? What was the big secret?

I didn't know the answers to any of these questions but I was absolutely certain about one thing.

She'd been to see Phil.

Suddenly I hated Phil Brady with all my heart.

Now I hate him with my lungs, my liver, my kidneys and my spleen as well.

Especially my spleen, because that's supposed to be the source of spite in your body. As in 'to vent one's spleen'.

I wish I could vent *my* spleen on Phil Brady.

I was right. Mum had nipped out for a rendezvous with him. He had something important to tell her. Something he'd found out over the weekend.

He's discovered Will's been missing training for the County game.

Will's in so much trouble. He's in trouble with Mum, he's in trouble at school. The only one he's not in trouble with is Dad. Yet.

I saw Phil laying into Will when I took the register back to the office. I wondered what on earth was going on. I discovered later if Mum could have got to him first she would have but she had an early start that Monday morning and was out before we were up for school.

Will was standing outside his classroom, his back against the wall. He looked as if he was pinned there by Phil who was towering over him, one hand against the wall, while the index finger of the other jabbed at Will. I could hear Phil's voice rising and falling as I came along the corridor. Words like 'devious' and 'wasted opportunities' and 'lies' and 'so disappointed' wafted down to me. I stopped in front of them.

'And what do you think your father's going to say about all this?' said Phil. Will stood silent, his eyes fixed on the floor. He looked pale but inscrutable. He'd shut down, I could tell. It was pointless going on at him because you wouldn't get through, but Phil didn't know that. Phil lost his temper and slammed his hand against the wall. I jumped but Will merely blinked hard.

'Look at me when I'm talking to you! Don't you think your mother's got enough to cope with at the moment without having to worry about you?'

Will looked up at Phil, his eyes veiled. 'Yessir.' His eyes moved to me and he looked back down again at the floor. Phil turned to me.

'Did you know about this?'

'What?'

'He's been missing practices for the league game on Friday nights. He's missed them all bar the first one.

He's been in hospital, according to him.'

It was my turn to look at the floor.

'You knew, didn't you?' Phil stared at me, his mouth open. 'I wondered what you were up to with those bogus French lessons.' He shook his head. 'I'm surprised at you, Spider, I really am. I thought rugby mattered to you.'

'It does! You know it does!'

'So why didn't you tell me what was going on? Why didn't you tell your mum?'

I looked at Will. His mask had slipped now I was being yelled at too. He was chewing his lip like he did when he was trying not to cry.

'He's my brother. I'm not going to split on him.'

Phil swore under his breath. 'No, you'd rather shut up and let him throw away the best chance he'll ever have to play rugby for Cornwall.'

I swallowed. I know, it was awful. But what could I do?

'Words fail me. I wouldn't have put you down as the jealous type, Spider.'

'What? I'm not jealous of Will!'

'You sure about that?' Phil turned away in disgust. 'This isn't finished yet, not by a long chalk. Now get back to your classrooms, the pair of you, before I say something I'll regret.' Will slunk away and I continued on my way to the office, register in hand, my spine rigid with fury.

'Spider?' I turned. Phil Brady was still standing in the same place, watching me.

'What?' How dare he suggest I was pleased Will had blown his chances. I was the one who'd tried to stop him!

'Why did he do it?'

I couldn't speak, my pride was stinging so much. 'Ask Will.'

Phil was right about one thing though. It wasn't finished yet. Will and I still had Mum to face. And Dad.

We walked home together after school, trying to work out how to handle this.

'How did he find out?' I asked.

'He went along to the training session on Friday to see how I was getting on.'

'Damn. That's why we trained on Monday last week. He said he had something he wanted to do on Friday. I just assumed he had a hot date with the French teacher.'

'She's history.'

I stared at him blankly. 'No, she's definitely French. It's Miss Watkins . . .'

'No, I mean she's yesterday's news. He's dumped her apparently. Got a new model.'

I felt my skin tingle, like hundreds of tiny ants were crawling all over it.

'Who?'

'How should I know? Becky told me at rehearsal.'

She hadn't told me. Because she wasn't talking to me, that's why. Will went on.

'Anyway, I wasn't there, was I? And they told him I hadn't been for ages, because I'd been in hospital.'

'Flipping heck. Did he tell them you were lying through your teeth?'

'I don't know. He was livid with me. He said I'd made him look a fool, I'd let him down and myself down and Dad down too.'

For a brief bizarre moment I had a picture of a washing line with three coloured balloons tied on it with string, bobbing about in the breeze, one with Will's face, one with Dad's face and one with Phil Brady's face. And the biggest, roundest, most inflated of them all was Dad's face, puffed up with pride.

I suppose Will must have been thinking the same sort of stuff because he suddenly stopped in his tracks and said, 'Oh, Spider! What do you think Dad will do when he finds out?'

'I dunno. You should have thought about that before.'

I knew what he'd do; so did Will. He'd rant and rave and yell blue murder. He'd ground Will, and me too probably, then he'd forbid Will to have anything to do with the show. And that's for starters.

I put my arm round Will and gave him a hug. 'Come on, kiddo, let's go home and try and sort this out.'

Mum was watching out for us; she must have finished early and it was obvious she meant business. The front door opened before we got there and she stood there glaring, her hands on her hips. She practically grabbed Will by the scruff of the neck and pushed him into the house ahead of her.

'You–ly–ing–lit–tle–git!' she chanted, punctuating each syllable with a vicious jab in his back with her finger. She flung him into a chair and stood over him, her eyes ablaze with fury, spitting questions at him without waiting for an answer. 'What do you think you're playing at? How could you throw away a chance to play for the County? What's your dad going to say about this?'

Then she turned on me. 'Did *you* know about this? Did *you* put him up to it?'

'This is nothing to do with me!' I yelled back, stung to the quick. 'Why is everyone trying to put the blame on me?'

Mum stopped to take breath and looked at me with narrowed eyes. You could almost hear the brain processes ticking over as she worked out I'd own up if I'd had anything to do with it. So she turned her attention back to Will and laid into him again, this time firing at him the sanctions she was going to impose on him. He was grounded (likely); she was placing him under lock and key (unlikely); she was stopping his pocket money (harsh) and numerous other far more inventive-but-impossible-to-carry-out-without-being-reported-to-Childline threats.

It was only what we expected and soon, I thought, she'll run out of steam. But all of a sudden, she stopped shouting and sat down heavily, taking us both by surprise. 'How could you?' she whispered and started blubbing into her hanky. Will, who I thought had taken the onslaught like a man up to now, looked at me in alarm and tried to sneak off but Mum snapped, 'Stay there!' and he subsided into the chair and waited till she'd stopped sobbing, which took absolutely ages. At last to my relief she got the hiccups and I went to fetch her a glass of water. She took a few sips then gave a huge sigh and blew her nose and peered at Will out of puffy red eyes.

'As if we didn't have enough to worry about at the moment,' she said. 'Why did you do it?'

So slowly and hesitantly, Will started to explain all about *A Plague on Your Town*. He described it in detail and as he went on his voice grew in confidence and his eyes shone and his face lit up, and anyone with half a brain could see how important it was to him. Mum sat there sceptical at first but soon you could tell she was drawn in and by the time he'd finished her eyes were soft and she looked as if she might start crying again.

'Come here, you,' she said.

Will went and sat next to her and then she did the thing women always do to Will, she went soft on him. She pushed his hair out of his eyes, then she smiled at him, a watery little smile with a sniff in the middle of it and a quivering chin, but a smile nevertheless. I don't know how he does it, I really don't.

'I thought you liked playing rugby,' she said.

'I do. But I like singing and dancing better,' said Will simply, as if that was all there was to it. 'And I couldn't do both at the same time. And the show will be over soon so I can get back to rugby then . . .'

'And you would never have found out if Phil Brady hadn't told you,' I finished off. I was still smarting at Phil's jibe about me being jealous of Will. And I would never get over him wrecking Dad's life.

'Phil just beat the rush. I was bound to hear about it sooner or later. I don't know how on earth you've managed to keep it a secret till now.'

'It's not long now. I'm really good, Mum. Let me do it then I promise I'll work hard at rugby and represent Cornwall and make you really proud of me. I will, honest.'

'I am proud of you, you idiot.' Mum put her arms round Will and hugged him so tightly he looked alarmed.

'Are you going to tell Dad?' he asked, face squashed up against her neck. She let him go and looked at him sadly.

'I'm going to have to, Will. You can't do things behind his back.' Tears welled up in Will's blue eyes.

'You do!'

Mum looked up at me, startled. 'What do you mean?'

'A small matter of a women's rugby team. Nights out training with the Botox Babes.'

'That's different!'

'Dad won't think so!'

Mum bit her lip. 'Okay, I agree, it's not right he's been kept in the dark. I'll tell him everything, but not just yet, he's got too much on his plate at the moment.'

A single tear trembled on Will's lower lid and splashed over to roll slowly down his cheek. Mum groaned. 'Oh sod it, it's too late to let everyone down. A couple of weeks and this damn show will be over and then you're back to training, right?'

'Right!'

'In the meantime, just say your prayers that your father doesn't find out till I've worked out a way to tell him. And don't you DARE pull a stunt like this again. EVER!'

Will's got off with it. The jammy so-and-so.

* ★ ★

On Wednesday Dad came home early so he could come with me and Mum to Parents' Evening. Normally I hate these, so I usually manage to lose the appointment form until most of the slots have gone, but tonight I had it all filled up at ten-minute intervals. I was hoping Mum and Dad would be in for a surprise. Mum made Will come too.

'I want you where I can see you,' she said. Will sighed but did as he was told. Mum was holding all the cards at the moment.

'You'd better go and wash and change,' she said to Dad who was watching the news after tea. 'We don't want to be late.' Dad glanced down at his work jeans, about to protest, but took one look at Mum and changed his mind. She looked amazing. Since she'd been training she'd been steadily losing weight and was now toned and slender. She was wearing tight trousers and a fitted jacket that showed off her figure, and her hair was as immaculate as ever.

'Is that get-up new?' asked Dad.

'Ish,' she said, as she peered in the mirror to put the final touches to her make-up. 'There, that'll do.' She sprayed herself with perfume and snapped her bag shut. 'I'm ready.'

Dad ran a hand over his bristles. 'I didn't know it was

a flaming fashion parade. I'll go and have a shave.'

When we walked into school that night the display was the first thing we saw in the entrance foyer. I'd spent the day putting it up with Janine, getting out of lessons to do so, much to everyone else's annoyance. People were gathered around it, reading the boards. There was lots of interest in the section on women's rugby and also in the stuff about the Tinners.

'Look, Dad, you're up there.' Will pointed to a team photo of the club from the eighties I'd borrowed from Gran's prize wall in her front room, the one when they'd won the County Cup. They were kneeling on the grass and Dad, the captain, was in the centre of the photo, holding the ball. He looked young and fit with a big grin on his face. I could see what Mum saw in him: even with the dodgy mullet, he was the best-looking bloke on the team.

'Did you do all this, Charlie?' He read through the stuff I'd been working on for weeks with interest. 'It's really good.'

I grinned with satisfaction. All my hard work had been worth it.

Various guys came up and identified themselves in the photo, though I would never have recognised these middle-aged men from the young faces on the team. They all shook hands with Dad and he stood there talking rugby with them, hands in his pockets. He's a bit of a local celebrity, my dad. I felt the familiar stirring of pride, but when Phil Brady came over and joined in the conversation, I stiffened. Would he tell Dad that Will wasn't turning up for training? No, of course he wouldn't. He'd told Mum in secret.

How could Dad be civil to him? I wouldn't if he'd shattered my leg and my dreams. Then I wondered why all these other guys were bothering to pass the time of day with him too, because some of them must have been around when it happened. I stood watching them all. Funny to think each one was a rugby champion in the past, but now they were just someone's dad.

Suddenly, I saw Dad in a different light, like he was someone I'd just come across for the first time. You see, up to that moment I think in my mind I'd always seen him like he was up on that board, a superhuman rugby legend. But he wasn't any more. He was middle-aged and it showed.

He'd bought himself a beer belly with all the drinking he'd been doing lately. Mum was always on at him about it but up till now he'd scrubbed up well. When he went out to rugby dinners dressed up in his club tie and blazer, he'd always looked what Gran called 'hunky'.

Not any more. Now that beer belly had grown so full of itself it was refusing to co-operate. It protruded over his belt and beyond the confines of his rugby blazer which was stretched, tight and shiny, across his back. His hair was thinning too, whether he'd admit it or not, and his face looked tired with bags under his eyes and jowly bits under his chin.

And next to him Phil Brady looked fit and strong and still young, even though I knew he was about the same age as my dad.

And immediately I felt *so* mean as if I'd betrayed my dad for Phil.

I caught sight of Mum. What a difference all that training and running had made.

She'd finished looking at the display and was waiting for Dad. She stood there patiently while he was talking, in her trendy jacket and her high-heeled boots, bag slung over her shoulder. She looked really pretty standing there in a world of her own with her arms folded, slim and smart and beautifully made up.

Then, Phil turned round and I saw him looking her up and down and I knew he was thinking the same as me. He likes her, it's obvious.

Don't even think about it, pal. She's my mum and she's happily married. And you've got a new girlfriend.

He caught her eye. Slowly and deliberately he winked at her.

She wrinkled her nose and smiled back.

And then it hit me like a physical pain, as if I'd been kicked in the guts and I gasped.

They couldn't be. Could they?

Mum said, 'Charlotte, are you all right?' I took a deep breath and grabbed hold of my spirited imagination as it whirled around and got it back under control.

'We'd better go in,' I said. 'Come on, Dad.' And we went through to the hall which was already teeming with reluctant kids and anxious parents. Around the edges teachers sat at individual tables, their names and subjects displayed before them and, in front of each table chairs sat waiting for their victims. A faint smell of stale school dinners lingered over the proceedings and, though I knew I had nothing to fear this time, I felt a bit queasy.

'These places never change,' said Dad uneasily, undoing the top button of his shirt. Mum took the appointment sheet out of her bag and consulted it. Some of the teachers had already started their interviews and queues were forming in front of the desks.

'Maths first,' said Mum.

Dad sniffed and squared his shoulders. 'See if we've been getting our money's worth from Phil Brady.'

Mum glared at him. 'Don't mention the coaching, he's not supposed to be doing it. And do your collar up!' she hissed then smiled sweetly at Dale the Fail as she sat down. I glanced at his file, open on the desk before me and relaxed. My grades spoke for themselves. Old Dale was charm itself, smarming his way round Mum and Dad with his declarations of glee at how much I'd improved in maths this term, taking all the credit for himself.

'Keep it up, Charlotte.' His piggy little eyes leered at me over the top of his glasses. 'We'll make a mathematician out of you yet.'

I don't think so, Slimeball.

We went from desk to desk to meet all my teachers and each one had something good to say about me for the first time since I'd been in the school.

'Come on in leaps and bounds, she has.'
'Huge improvement in attitude.'
'Trying really hard.'
'Pulling her weight at last.'
'She's made real progress this term.'
'A pleasure to have in the classroom.'

One after the other they sang my praises and Mum and Dad stared at me in shock as if they'd discovered a changeling in their midst. You could almost see Dad swelling with pride and Mum was beaming from ear to ear. For once Will, who was trailing round after us, didn't get a look in.

I should have been over the moon, me getting the

accolades for once. I deserved it, I really did. I'd been giving a hundred and ten per cent this term since the day Phil Brady had picked me for the Tag Rugby team. It was as if he'd knocked on my door and when I answered it he'd walked straight into my life to show me that anything is possible.

The trouble is, I think he's had the same effect on my mother.

I had to talk to Becky. I didn't care that she wasn't speaking to me because I'd called her boyfriend a maggot in a sheep's bum. I didn't care that she was spending every available spare minute in the maggot's company. I had to find out about Phil Brady's new girlfriend.

'Who is she?'

'What's it to you?'

'I just wondered, that's all.'

'Why you asking me?'

'Will said you'd seen her.'

Becky shrugged. She didn't look as if she was keeping something from me, something important like, 'It's your mum but obviously I can't tell you that.' She looked more like, 'Who the hell do you think you are, ignoring me for a fortnight then interrogating me like this?'

We were on the school field waiting for Phil to turn up for training. I'd been trying to get this daft idea out of my head ever since Parents' Evening. Mum and Dad were so made up to hear how well I was doing they seemed to have forgotten their differences and all was peaceful in the house, like the old days. Calm before the storm as it turned out, but I didn't know that then.

Mum was jogging round the edge of the school field with the oldies. I'd spotted Becky sitting on the steps of the cricket pavilion and had gone over to join her.

'I don't know much. Wayne and I were out on Saturday night and I saw him going into a pub with his arm around a woman. It was dark and I only saw the back of her, but it definitely wasn't Miss Whatsername from your school, she was too short.'

'What did she look like?'

'I just said, I couldn't see her properly. I don't know, middle-aged, ordinaryish. They all look the same at that age, don't they? Sort of like your mum or mine. What's it to you anyway?' Becky stared at me then her jaw dropped. 'You fancy him, don't you? You've got the hots for Phil!'

'Puh-lease! He's old enough to be my dad!' I was about to put her straight on that score when I managed to stop myself just in time. Better she should think I fancied him than there was something going on between Mum and him. Because I'd just remembered Mum had gone out for a drink on Saturday night, with the 'girls' from work she'd said.

But Becky would have recognised Mum, surely? She would, wouldn't she? In the dark? From the back? Maybe not. My imagination leapt up to start zipping round again but I squashed it firmly down and changed the subject.

'How's Dobbin . . . I mean Wayne?'

'All right.' Becky's face took on a closed look, wary. 'Why?'

'No reason.' I took a deep breath. 'I'm sorry I called him you-know-what. And I'm sorry I tried to put you off him, Becks. There's loads of baggage between . . . Wayne . . . and me. We go back a long way.'

'I know, he told me.' She was silent for a minute, thinking, then she said, 'I know he can be a pain, Spider, but I like him, I can't help it.' She sighed and nodded meaningfully. 'You can't control who you fall for, you should know that.' I turned to see what she was looking at. Phil's car had just pulled into the car park. I bit my tongue to stop myself protesting and smiled weakly. How the hell did I get myself into this?

We had a great training session. We were all pretty fit by now so we got through the circuit training quickly and went on to skills. Phil had brought along a load of plastic water bottles and he taught us how to juggle with them to improve our handling techniques. It was fun.

We kids caught on quickly and by the end of the session most of us could manage three bottles. The oldies were dreadful, no one getting past two, though there was a lot of cursing and shrieking.

We finished off with a game, twenty minutes each way, Under Fourteens against the Seniors. It was a close-run thing but we managed to hang on to the victory with Freya bringing Marlene down in a brilliant covering tackle in the last minutes of the game. I can't believe Freya's the same girl who, when we first started, used to squeal if she got her hands dirty. She's improved so much. We all have, I guess.

At the end Phil said he wanted to speak to us. We pulled our tracksuits on and sprawled on the grass, chests heaving, breath rising in white clouds into the night air.

'Right, I've got some news for you. I've got some fixtures booked.'

We all sat up as one man. One woman!

'Seniors, there's a new team started up Plymouth way. They're not quite ready yet but they're getting there. I've booked a game on their ground mid-February. It's just a friendly so we don't have to worry too much about numbers.'

The women buzzed with excitement, all except Mum who seemed to know about it already.

'Now then, you Under Fourteens.' You could tell Phil

was excited, though he was pretending to be cool. 'Ready for this? We've been invited to take part in an exhibition match before the County game on Christmas Eve.'

There was a stunned silence. I found my voice first as usual. 'I thought the County game was at the end of January,' I said. 'Will's playing in the exhibition match before it.' My voice tailed off as Phil raised his eyebrows at me and said, 'Really?'

Then he went on. 'That's Devon. But Somerset is playing against us Christmas Eve and they've got a brand-new Under Fourteens Girls' side looking for a match. I reckon you're ready to show them a thing or two.'

'All of us?' said Freya. 'Do you mean all of us?'

'Freya, do you really think I'd leave you out after you brought Marlene the Mighty crashing to the ground?'

'Oi, less of the Mighty. I've lost two stone since we started this malarkey!' Marlene boomed indignantly. We all laughed then we cheered and hugged each other. It was going to happen at last, it really was.

That night Mum and I jogged home together under the stars and I felt as if they were shining just for me. My dream had come true. I would represent my County at rugby.

'Can I tell Dad now?'

'Yes,' said Mum. 'It's time.'

When we got home Dad was already in. He was slumped on the sofa, feet up, watching television, and he hadn't even bothered to take his shoes off. The pile of empty cans on the floor beside him suggested he'd been there for some time.

'Dad?'

He grunted.

'Dad. I've got something to tell you.'

'Where the hell have you two been?' he said, not even bothering to look up. Mum frowned. Oh no. They'd been getting on so much better since Parents' Evening. Don't start, the pair of you.

'We went out for a run. We're trying to keep fit in case you hadn't noticed.' She knocked his feet off the sofa and sat down next to him. 'You're home early.'

Dad took a long swig till he'd emptied his can, then he crushed it in his fist and belched. Mum's face darkened.

'Not much point in grafting if you're not being paid for it.'

'What do you mean, you're not being paid for it?'

Dad got unsteadily to his feet and went out to the kitchen, returning with yet another can. He pulled the ring off and glugged it down his throat before sitting heavily back down again and staring moodily at the television.

'Do you mind telling me what's going on? I'm not a flipping mind-reader you know.'

'Scotts have pulled out.'

'What do you mean they've pulled out?' Mum's face was perplexed. Scotts was the building firm Dad was fitting the kitchens and bathrooms for. They were the reason he'd been working all hours of the day and night for weeks on end. The reason we'd taken out another loan on top of remortgaging the house.

'They've gone bust! Into liquidation! Belly up! Wiped out! Bloody bankrupt! How many other ways do you want me to say it!' Dad took another gulp from his can then hurled it into the fireplace. A tile cracked where it landed and beer dripped down into the grate. 'Happy now?' he said.

'That's not fair,' said Mum, her face white with shock.

'Too bloody right,' said Dad. The doorbell rang, making me jump, and I went to open it. Will stood there.

'I forgot my key.'

'Watch out,' I warned. 'Dad's on the warpath.'

We went back in the lounge where Mum and Dad were still sitting in silence. Will sat down, picked up a magazine and pretended to read it. After a while Dad raised his eyes to look at him blearily.

'All right, son?' he asked. 'How was training?'

Will's eyes flicked from Mum to me and back again. 'Not bad.'

'Looks as if I can get along to watch you now,' Dad sighed. 'Every cloud and all that.'

Will looked alarmed. 'What?'

'Your dad's run into a spot of bother with his business,' said Mum, shaking her head at him imperceptibly. 'Nothing for you to worry about.'

'Nothing for you to worry about . . .' exploded Dad. 'I'll remind you of that when they chuck us all out on the street.' He got up and grabbed his coat from the end of the stairs. 'I'm out of this.' The front door slammed shut behind him.

There was silence. I could feel my heart thudding against my ribcage. Will was as still as a statue, staring fixedly at the floor. Mum sat with her arms pressed tight against her ribs, gnawing at her knuckles, lost in her own thoughts. At last she gave a big sigh and looked up.

'It's not going to come to that,' she said. 'So don't you two worry your heads about it.'

Easier said than done, Mum. That night in bed I felt as if all the individual bags of dread I'd been carrying about in my head had burst open and the contents had come tumbling out and were now scrambled together in a whirlpool of worry. There was no start and no end to them, just a swirling vortex of fear.

Will misses rugby training; Dad will kill him when he finds out. Gran's losing her mind; who will look after her? Dobbin and Becky, sitting in a tree; two little love birds, what about me? Dad, stop arguing with Mum; can't you see you're driving her away? Your business is collapsing; we'll be out on the streets next. Ladybird, ladybird, fly away home; your house is on fire, your children are gone.

I'm going mad.

When I wake up next morning, my pillow is wet.

Mum went off to work as usual but Dad stayed in bed till lunchtime. He looked blotchy and unkempt when he got up and he didn't want anything to eat, just a couple of mugs of black coffee. After a while he went and put his coat on.

'Come on then. We'll miss the start if we don't get a move on.'

Yes! It was like old times! We got to the ground with minutes to spare and made our way to the stand. Blokes spoke to Dad or slapped him on the shoulder as we edged past them to our seats. I felt the familiar stirring of pride. He was well thought of in rugby circles, my dad. For a minute, I thought about telling him I was going to play for the County, he'd be so made up. Then I glanced at Will. I hadn't had a chance to tell him yet. I'd better not spring it on Dad now, it might make it awkward for Will. Dad would be bound to start boasting about his brilliant kids, both representing the County. Better say nothing at the moment. Anyway, the game was about to begin.

The Tinners got off to a good start and settled down well. They soon took the lead with a fine penalty followed by a drop goal. In the second half they lost pace for a while, but after they yielded a try which was quickly converted, they battled back to take two further penalties and win the game.

'Good job the fly-half had his kicking boots on,' said Dad as we filed out of the ground. 'Otherwise we'd have lost the match.'

'They could have done with a bit of your pace on the wing, Bob.' Phil Brady, at Dad's elbow, smiled at us. 'Good to see these two following in your footsteps.'

'What? Our Will, you mean?'

'And Spider. You must be proud of them both.'

Dad stared after Phil as he shouldered his way out of the ground.

'Weird bloke,' he said. 'What the hell's he on about, Charlie?'

I looked at my dad. His face was pinched and blue with cold except where a web of red veins marked his nose and cheeks and his lip was curled in a sneer. I didn't want to tell him, not like this. I'd save it for a better day.

'Nothing, Dad,' I said. 'Nothing important.'

'I'll be back tomorrow night,' said Mum, laying her best fluffy jumper neatly in her overnight bag. 'There's a lasagne in the freezer and a salad in the fridge.'

'Yes, Mum.'

'Don't forget to go round your gran's after school tonight and see if she needs anything. There's no training so you'll have plenty of time.'

'Yes, Mum.'

'And keep an eye on that brother of yours.'

'Yes, Mum.'

She looked at me quizzically. 'Are you trying to be sarcastic?'

'No!'

'Sorry. Difficult to tell sometimes. Not a word to your dad now. As far as he's concerned I'm at a beauty conference in Bath with Marlene.'

'When are you going to tell him the truth?'

'When I get a civil word out of him and not before.'

A car hooted impatiently in the street outside and she placed her mobile on the top of her jumper and zipped up her bag with a flourish. 'That's me. I'm out of here!'

Mum was off for a sleepover with Phil. No, I'm joking. She was going away on a course with Phil, Marlene, and Bev, the four main committee members, to do with administration, registration, affiliation and all those other 'ation' words you need to set up a women's team. She and Marlene were closing the salon early and driving there in Marlene's new little convertible. What was that film? *Thelma and Louise!* The next time we saw them would probably be on the *Six O'clock News* with their hands above their heads surrounded by armed police.

Phil was going to pick up Bev after work and join them later. Between you and me, I was happy Mum was travelling up with Marlene; I think it would have been seriously weird to see her driving off for a weekend with Phil. Mum was excited at the prospect of a night away, even if it was just talking rugby rules. To be honest, I think she was thrilled to be getting away from Dad who was like a grizzly bear with a migraine.

All week he'd lived a Jekyll and Hyde existence. He was either slobbing round the house, watching daytime TV and cursing Scotts, or he was rushing off to business meetings with the bank, crammed into his wedding suit (lapels too thin, trousers too narrow) and reeking of the dodgy aftershave Will had bought him three Christmases ago. Either way, he'd been a pain to live with.

He'd spent the evenings stuck in front of the computer doing money calculations and swearing under his breath. On Thursday night Mum said, 'Phil will be round soon to help Charlotte with her maths. Why don't you ask him to give you a hand?' and then he swore *over* his breath, loudly and profusely, and went out to the pub, slamming the door behind him.

I could tell Mum was really fed up with him; we all were. And I still hadn't told him about me playing on Christmas Eve because there was no talking to him when he was in that sort of mood.

I wish I were the one who was going away.

I called in to Gran's after school, like Mum asked. She was really hyper, up and down all the time like she couldn't be still and chatting away nineteen to the dozen.

'She's wearing me out,' said Gramps wearily. 'She's been going on about the Tinners since the minute she got up.'

'Going to watch the Tinners tomorrow?' she asked me, right on cue.

'Spect so, Gran. You coming?'

'I'll be there as usual,' she said.

Gramps shook his head at me but he didn't need to.

I knew she hadn't set foot in the ground this season.

When I got home that night Dad had made an effort. He had the table laid and the lasagne heating up in the oven. Well, the table was half laid for three, the other half was spread with newspaper and he was polishing his shoes on it. He was whistling in his own individual tuneless way and seemed happy for once.

Will was sitting at the table watching him, his chin in his hands. He seemed very *un*happy. I could feel the anxiety burning from him, like a distress flare.

'Tea won't be long,' said Dad, buffing his shoes till they shone. 'I thought I'd go along to watch our Will training tonight.'

Will's eyes flashed at me for help. It was the dress rehearsal tonight, there was no way he could miss it. Mayday! Mayday!

I took a deep breath. Lifeboat to the rescue.

'Oh no! That means I'll be all on my own!'

Dad stopped buffing and looked at me in surprise. 'Come with us then.'

'I can't,' I whined. 'I've got homework.'

'Give over, Charlie,' said Dad, resuming his polishing. I swear he could see his face in those shoes. 'It's Friday night.'

'I've got loads to do.' My voice rose a notch. 'I don't want to fall behind.'

Dad looked at me irritably. 'Well, you stay here and do it then. We won't be long.'

'I don't like being on my own.' My voice trembled. Was I overdoing it? I wasn't such a good actor as Will.

'It might go on a bit,' said Will, picking up the thread at last. 'Mum wouldn't like her being left in the house on her own. You stay with Spider, Dad, I don't mind, honest.'

I'll bet you don't, you little toerag. Dad chucked the duster on the floor and gave me a look of disgust. Who could blame him? Go to the rugby ground and watch your wonderful son, the pride of your loins, train with the cream of the County or stay home and watch your nerdy wuss of a daughter do her homework. No contest!

'You owe me!' I hissed at Will as Dad stamped upstairs to put his sparkling shoes away. My reward was an equally dazzling beam of gratitude. Huh!

Once Will had gone I had to do the washing up because Dad had gone into a big sulk. Then I had to get my flipping books out and pretend to be absorbed in them while Dad watched live rugby league on *Sky Sports*. Funny thing was, eventually I did get down to my maths and I was actually ploughing through my number sequences when the phone rang. It was Granddad.

'Spider, love. Is your dad there?'

'Yeah. Is anything wrong?'

There was a pause. 'She's gone again. I've had a look

outside but there's no sign of her. I think she might have gone into town.'

Oh no. I held the phone out to Dad. 'Gran's gone missing again.'

Dad sprang up and barked into the phone for a while then grabbed his coat and keys. 'Come on then. I can't leave you on your own, can I?' I stuck my tongue out at his departing back and followed him. At least it wasn't raining this time.

'Gramps seems to think she might have gone shopping.' We cruised up and down the high street, strung with a sad line of Christmas lights now, but there was no sign of an old lady with her shopping bag, just grown-ups out celebrating the end of a working week and gangs of kids hanging round shop doorways. 'Where the hell can she be?' Dad pulled the van into the kerb and took out his mobile. 'I'll ring your mum. She might have some idea where she could have got to. Where's she staying, Charlie?'

'I don't know. Somewhere in Bath.'

'That's helpful. Never mind, I'll get her on her mobile.'

He'd pulled her number up on his list and pressed the button before it occurred to me this might not be such a good idea. I cast around desperately for something to stop him.

'Don't trouble her, Dad. She can't do anything and

she'll only worry.' Dad nodded as if he was about to press the off button but it was too late.

'Trace?' Dad's face went blank for a moment and he actually pulled his phone away from his ear and looked at it before putting it back and repeating, 'Tracy, is that you?'

'Wrong number?' I said helpfully.

'Wrong bloody person,' he said. My heart sank. He started tearing at his thumbnail savagely with his teeth then Mum must have come on the line because he exploded.

'Tracy? Who the bloody hell was that?'

Mum's voice could be heard in the background, tinny and reedy, but I couldn't catch what she was saying. I didn't need to though. One side of the conversation was enough.

'Phil? Phil who?' Comprehension dawned in his eyes. 'Phil (very rude word, very, very rude word, followed by the rudest word I'd ever heard) Brady? What the hell is he doing at a (that word again) beauty conference?'

I squeezed my eyes tight shut and sank down in my seat, my fingers pressed to my ears to block out the choice expletives Dad was yelling down the phone. At last I became aware that he'd stopped and I cautiously opened my eyes. He was staring through the windscreen, his face like thunder, and tapping his phone against the steering wheel at the same time. I released my ears. Tap, tap, tap, tap, on and on, like some crazy kind of Morse code.

'Dad?'

He turned to me, eyes blazing, his face twisted with fury. 'Did you know about this?'

I stared at him, not knowing what to say. He grabbed me by the wrist so tightly it hurt. 'Did you?' he spat at me.

I burst into tears.

He let me go, slamming my arm back and it cracked against the door. I howled, clutching my elbow in my other hand. Dad looked horrified.

'I'm sorry, Charlie, I'm sorry. I didn't mean to do that. I'm sorry, love.' He put his arms round me and half patted, half rubbed my back and this made me cry more. 'It's not your fault, I shouldn't be taking it out on you. Even if you did know what was going on, none of this is your fault.'

'Nothing *is* going on,' I hiccuped, but it was a lie. I didn't know that for sure. It was all so horrible. I sobbed into his shirt like a baby. I could feel his chest rising and falling as he breathed and his heart beating, fast at first, then gradually slowing down, and this steadied me and finally I stopped crying.

'You've soaked me,' he said and I managed a watery

smile. He took out his hanky and wiped my eyes. 'Come on, blow your nose like a good girl and we'll go and find your gran.' I blew my nose obediently, four years old again, and he started up the van and swung it round. 'I've had an idea. We'll try the town hall; she might think it's Monday Club again.'

Call me stupid but I never gave it a thought. I was just glad Dad had calmed down and we had something *normal* to do like look for Gran together. (It wasn't normal a few months ago, when she went missing the first time; it was awful then, but everything's relative, I've discovered.) So it never crossed my mind that's where Will would be.

We pulled up outside the hall. Tonight it was ablaze with light and kids were spilling down the steps, chatting and laughing.

'What's going on here?' asked Dad, getting out of the van. 'Have they got a show on or something?'

Too late I realised as I got out to join him on the pavement. Rehearsal had finished, the big one, the dress rehearsal, before the actual show next Friday. There was a big banner advertising it above the door.

'*A Plague on Your Town,*' read Dad. 'It's on next weekend. Our Will would like to see that, I bet.'

And right on cue, the little trouper that he is, my kid brother appeared at the front door with Becky, as if they were stepping into the spotlight. They were laughing and joking and as we watched, Becky shouted, 'There's my bus! See you next week!' and ran off down the steps and across the road. Will watched as she disappeared out of sight then shifted his rugby bag on his shoulder and bounded down the steps, two at a time, not looking where he was going. The last four steps he took together and jumped, landing in a sprawl at our feet. He looked up and his face transposed itself into a comic mask of horror.

'In the van,' said Dad. 'Now!'

He opened the passenger door, staring grimly at Will. My brother hung back, waiting for me to get in first so he wouldn't have to sit next to Dad but Dad grabbed hold of his collar and the elastic round his trackie pants and bundled him in. I scrambled in after him and Dad slammed the door. I just had time to warn Will, 'Watch out. All hell's let loose,' before Dad opened the driver's door and swung himself into his seat. Will shrank back but Dad gave him a look of disgust, clicked his tongue against his teeth and we continued home in silence.

When we got home we trooped in and Will made to escape upstairs.

'Sit there,' Dad barked. 'I haven't got time to deal with you yet.' He picked up the phone and dialled Gramps. 'She's not come back? Okay, I'm calling the police.' I could hear Granddad protesting on the end of the line but Dad was adamant. 'No, Dad, it's freezing out there and she could be anywhere. We need help. You stay put.'

It wasn't long before the police arrived on our doorstep, a copper called Steve, who used to play for the Tinners with Dad, and a policewoman. They took all the details quickly and methodically, then Steve radioed the information through to the switchboard.

'They're sending a couple of cars out straight away, Bob. We'll find your mum in next to no time. Don't you worry, this happens more often than you'd think and they always turn up somewhere safe and sound.'

'We'll go round to your father's in the meantime and check up on things there,' added the policewoman. 'We'll be in contact as soon as we know anything.'

Dad came back into the lounge when the police had gone and glared at Will, sitting bolt upright on the sofa, and I thought, now for it, but he sat down suddenly and ran his fingers through his hair.

'Put the kettle on, Charlie. It looks as though we may be in for a long night.'

I don't know how many cups of tea I made over the next hours and in all that time Dad never said a word. He spent most of the time staring at the blank television screen and drumming his fingers, on and on. Once he took his mobile out and scrolled through and I thought, he's going to ring Mum again, but he changed his mind and threw it on the floor. After a while, Will's eyes drooped and his head slumped and then Dad got up and put a blanket over him.

'Go on up to bed, Charlie,' he said but I shook my head. I couldn't sleep till I knew that Gran was all right. Dad put his feet up on the coffee table, folded his arms and closed his eyes, but I knew he wasn't asleep either.

In the end we must have dozed off because when the police car pulled up outside our house Dad and I jumped up in shock, as the blue light rotated through our curtains and bounced off the walls of our lounge like the beam from a lighthouse. We were at the front door before the two coppers had time to get out of the car and put their hats on.

At the same time a car screeched to a halt behind the police car and a woman jumped out of the passenger seat.

'What's going on?' she screamed. 'What's happened?'
It was Mum.

Poor Mum. She had the shock of her life. She was already freaked out by Dad's phone call, so she'd persuaded Marlene to drive her home in the dead of night, only to be greeted by blazing lights, a police car and two coppers at the front door.

I ran to her. She hugged me and looked at Dad. Her face was as white as a sheet. 'It's not Will, is it? Tell me it's not Will.'

He shook his head. 'Will's fine,' he said. 'It's Mum. She's been missing all night.'

'Oh, Bob,' she said and threw her arms round him.

The policeman cleared his throat. I'd almost forgotten he was there.

'It's okay, we've found her. She's been taken to hospital for a check-up. She's confused and suffering from hypothermia but she should be all right. Your father's with her now.'

'Thank God for that.' Dad buried his face in Mum's hair and wrapped his arms round us both, squeezing us tight. When he let go he looked as if he'd done ten rounds with Mike Tyson and survived – just. 'Where did she get to?'

'You're never going to believe this,' the policewoman smiled. 'We'd tried everywhere and had run out of ideas. Then Steve here was talking about what a great character she was. He remembered how she loved her rugby; how she watched the Tinners every week. He said she used to run the line hurling abuse at the ref if he made a decision against you.'

'Aye, she did.' Dad tried to laugh but it came out like a sob.

'We decided to go down the ground to take a look,' continued Steve. 'When we got there a group of kids was hanging about outside. They ran off as soon as they saw us, then we noticed the lock was broken on the gates. They'd obviously broken in.

'We had a look round then tied up the gate. We were just leaving when one of them came back on his own.'

The policewoman picked up the story. 'He told us they'd been in earlier to kick a ball round. He said an old lady had followed them in and had sat in the stand watching them. She was still in there as far as he knew. He was worried about her.'

'We went in and had another look and then we found her. She was stretched out at the back of the stand, asleep. It's lucky that lad was concerned about her. She'd have frozen to death by the morning.'

'We can't thank him enough,' said Dad. 'What's his name?'

The policewoman checked her notes.

'Wayne Dobson.'

'I'll leave you to it,' said Marlene. 'You've got a lot to talk about.'

Mum hugged her tight, then we watched her and the police car drive away and went inside. When Mum caught sight of Will fast asleep on the sofa, looking as angelic and oblivious as ever, she sat down heavily as if her legs wouldn't support her any more and drew me to her.

'I've only been gone a day,' she said. 'What's been going on?'

'That's what I'd like to know,' said Dad.

We didn't go to bed at all that night. There wasn't much left of it and there was so much explaining to do. To be honest for a moment it did cross my mind Dad might grab Mum by the throat and interrogate her about what she was up to in Bath with Phil Brady on a Friday night but he didn't, thank God. It was as if, seeing her with Marlene, all his anger had dissipated and he was just relieved that she was back and Gran was found and was going to be okay.

And Mum wasn't mad at being dragged home from her precious weekend away either. It turned out to be really boring. 'I never knew there were so many rules and regulations to the game of rugby,' she said. 'If I'd had to listen to any more of them I'd have gone completely round the twist.'

She told Dad the whole story, no holds barred. 'I was fed up with Charlotte playing second fiddle to Will,' she explained. 'She was brilliant at the game, but you hardly noticed.'

I squirmed, feeling stupid. Was it that obvious? She looked at me sympathetically but carried on. 'That's how it all started. I decided to start up a women's team and Phil Brady agreed to be the coach. Now we've got two teams, Seniors and Under Fourteens. I play for the Seniors.' She stuck her chin out defiantly. Dad's face was a picture but wisely he refrained from commenting. 'We've been training for months now. Charlotte's got some news for you.'

I sat there as the grey morning light filtered through the crack in the curtains and told Dad that I was going to play against Somerset at the County Ground on Christmas Eve. He got *so* emotional. I swear there were tears in his eyes.

'Charlie, I never once thought of you as second best,' said Dad and his voice actually cracked. 'I'm really proud of you. Why didn't you tell me before?'

'You weren't listening.'

But now he was. They both were.

So, suddenly, it was like I'd popped a cork and all the worries bubbled out that I'd been keeping inside me for so long, silly stuff like Dobbin and Becky, and how they'd got off together and they didn't want me around and I thought I liked him and he liked me and what a horrible bloke he was and all that bunk.

And Dad said, 'Is this the same horrible bloke who went back and told the police about that little old lady sitting in the stand on a cold dark night, even though he could have got himself arrested? He saved your gran's life, Charlie.'

So that made *me* all emotional and I started blubbing (again) and Mum put her arms round me and said, 'What's the matter?' and I wailed, 'I don't want you to split up!'

'What makes you think we're going to split up?' asked Mum, bewildered.

'Because you're rowing all the time,' I sobbed, '. . . and Dad's lost his contract and . . .' My voice trailed away.

'And what? Out with it, Charlotte!'

'Phil Brady,' I whispered.

'PHIL BRADY? What's he got to do with it?'

'Sshh!' I tried to hush Mum but she was having none of it.

'Phil Brady? Surely you didn't think . . . ?'

I darted a look at Dad. He was watching Mum like a hawk. She started chuckling.

'Give me a break, Charlotte. If I was going to run away with someone it wouldn't be with another rugby fanatic. What do you think I am, a glutton for punishment? PHIL BRADY! Oh, wait till I tell Bev!'

What is Mum like when she sees the funny side of something? Once she starts laughing she can't stop; it's side-splitting stuff. Soon I was joining in giggling and when I looked at Dad he was smiling too.

Though I don't know if that was with relief.

Mum's convulsions woke Will up, he stirred and I saw his eyelids flickering, but he turned over and carried on playing dead, worried I suppose he was going to get it in the neck from Dad if he showed signs of life. After a while Mum sobered up and stroked my cheek apologetically.

'I'm sorry you thought that, sweetheart. See what we've been putting her through, Bob?'

Dad looked shame-faced. 'We have been having a go at each other lately, Trace.'

'Well, it's time we stopped.'

'It was my fault,' said Dad. 'I've been too wrapped up in the business.'

'No, it was mine,' said Mum. 'I've not been supportive enough.'

'Give it a rest,' I grumbled, shrugging Mum's arm off. 'You can't even agree whose fault it is. Anyway, why do you have to tell Bev what I thought?'

'Because *she's* trying her hardest to get off with Phil!'

'And you've left her alone with him!'

Mum and Dad grinned at each other in delight.

'Anyway, one thing's for sure, there'll be no more secrets in this family,' said Dad. He turned to regard his supposedly sleeping son on the sofa. 'So who's going to tell me what my fella here's been up to?'

Will's breathing suddenly became deep and regular.

Mum looked mortified. 'Do you know?'

'I don't know anything! Do you?' Dad looked hurt.

'I've only just found out myself. Charlotte, tell your father what Will's been doing.'

I hesitated, remembering how Mum had lost it when she found out. Dad would go ballistic. Then I looked at my brother pretending to sleep like a baby and thought, right, mate, if you won't tell them, I will, because there was no point in trying to keep it secret any longer. So I filled them in on how he wanted to be in the musical more than anything in the whole world to the extent that he'd fabricated this story about hospital so he wouldn't have to miss the rehearsals.

'He wrote a letter to the RFU pretending it was me?' repeated Dad, shaking his head in disbelief. 'The little blighter!'

At this point Will went into snoring mode but now he was fooling no one.

Poor Dad. He couldn't believe what he was hearing.

'I warned you not to push him so hard,' said Mum, but her eyes were full of concern for Dad.

'Doesn't he want to play rugby then?' he said, trying to get his head around it.

'Yes, of course he does. He just wants to go on the stage more.'

'I want to do both,' said Will, opening his eyes and proving how good his timing was. 'I can play rugby once the show is over.'

'You've got it all worked out, haven't you?'

'Sorry, Dad.' Will tried his abject sorrow look on Dad, the one where he peers up through his fringe and looks mournful but it didn't work.

Dad cuffed his ear and said, 'Don't give me that, you little waster. This isn't the end of the matter,' but when he stood up, I saw a glimmer of a smile on his lips.

Who'd have thought it?

I went upstairs to wash and change. What a night!

At least everything was out in the open now. All of a sudden I felt exhausted. As I was cleaning my teeth I got a text. It was from Becky and it was just one word.

'Mates?'

'Mates,' I texted back.

Mum cooked us all a big fry-up then we all piled in the van and went round to the hospital to see Gran. She was sitting up in bed chatting to the nurse. Granddad was asleep in the chair.

'She seems fine,' said the nurse. 'Tough as old boots this one. Once the doctor's done his rounds this afternoon I think she can go home. She's been telling me all about you, how her son plays for Cornwall. Do you still play?' she asked doubtfully, eyeing Dad.

'Not any more,' said Dad. 'But my daughter does.'

The town hall was crammed fit to bursting. All the seats were taken and officials were trying to move on people who were standing at the back and in the aisles, saying things like, 'You can't stand there,' and 'Fire risk!' and 'Have you got a ticket?' They just shuffled round though until they found a corner to squeeze themselves into then other people took their places. We'd come early to bag our seats but even so we were still halfway back.

I was in between Gran and Granddad. Gran was clutching a mountain of raffle tickets she'd bought on the way in. 'When's the raffle?' she asked.

'In the interval, Gran.' She looked lovely tonight, in her best coat, a blue silk scarf at her throat. We'd all scrubbed up well. Granddad looked back to his old self and Dad had on his best birthday sweatshirt, the one Phil had put on the day Mum washed his shirt for him. It looked nicer on Dad, if a little tight; the colour suited him better. Mum looked gorgeous in a new black leather jacket, an early Christmas present from Dad, and I had on a new pair of jeans and a skinny top, also from Dad, and I was feeling pretty good myself, I can tell you.

Because Dad's business has been saved. (Some big firm had bought Scotts out so the development was still going ahead.) No workhouse for us! Dad was like a dog with two tails.

The orchestra started tuning up, a real orchestra! This was just like a West End show! The lights dimmed and the music began, soft and slow at first, then building up to a rousing crescendo. At the end everyone clapped then silence fell as the curtains opened to reveal an old-fashioned scene, a village square, with an old water pump in the centre and a church painted on the backdrop. People mingled, the women in long skirts and bonnets, the men in trousers to the knee and shirts, greeting each other and chatting, then the story started unfolding.

It was a celebration and guess what they were celebrating? The engagement of my little brother Will to my bezzie, Becky. (Well, actually, it was the betrothal of Matthias to Arabella, the village beauty. Trust Becky!)

There was lots of back-slapping and bonhomie and singing and dancing, spurred on by a boy I recognised from Year 10 playing the fiddle. I didn't know he could do that! Will was really light on his feet. I'd never seen him dance before, not properly, whirling Arabella round as if there were no tomorrow.

Which there wasn't. Because no sooner were they betrothed and Matthias had gone back to his own village to till the soil and save up for his wedding than, lo and behold, Arabella's father gets sick and dies, quite spectacularly, with lots of loud vomiting and wailing and huge black boils on his face. (The make-up was amazing!) Then lots more people die, one after the other, including his baby son, and his wife buries him next to his father (really sad this, cue lots of mournful music from the orchestra). Gran started snivelling into her handkerchief so I held her hand and whispered, 'It's only a doll, Gran.'

Anyway, you've got it. The plague has come to the village and no one is allowed in or out, including poor lovesick Matthias who wants to rescue the lovely Arabella. So he hatches a cunning plan to save her and it's a race against time. By the time we get to the interval it looks as if Matthias is going to lose out to the grim reaper and Gran has lost all interest in the raffle and is bawling her head off.

Of course, everything turns out happily. Well, I suppose when your whole family has been wiped out by the plague, maybe 'happy ever after' is the wrong phrase to use for poor Arabella. But she rallies round when

Matthias sings to her (more sobbing from Gran and most of the female audience) and looks amazingly jolly, all things considered, as she dances a reel with him at her wedding. There are not a lot of villagers left at the end to join in the celebrations but then they all get miraculously resurrected and come on to take a bow and have a final jig together.

And there wasn't a dry eye in the house, as they say.

'That was brilliant,' said Mum, her face glowing with pride.

'Fantastic,' agreed Dad. 'I had no idea he was so talented.'

'I did enjoy that,' said Gran, dabbing her eyes with her hanky. 'Who was that boy who played Matthias? He was very good.'

It was my turn next. My moment of glory. Only the trouble was we were losing 66–0 and the crowd was on its feet booing us. My mother was weeping and my father was brandishing a shotgun and yelling, 'You're no daughter of mine!' As the whistle blew for the end of the game, he took aim and fired.

I sat bolt upright in bed, my heart thudding. What a nightmare! I'd taken hours to get to sleep and when I finally did I'd been besieged by unspeakable horrors all night long. On the wardrobe door hung my County sweatshirt, black and yellow stripes like a bumblebee. Folded neatly on my dressing table were my black shorts and socks and by the door my boots were waiting, polished to perfection last night by Dad. It was Christmas Eve.

Downstairs in the kitchen Dad was trying to cram a huge Tesco shop into the fridge; Mum was up to her elbows in flour. On the table, trays filled with pastry shells lay waiting for mincemeat amongst a scattering of cards still waiting to be put up.

'I'll just shove these in the oven then I'm off to do my shampoo and sets,' said Mum, ladling out generous spoonfuls. 'I'll be back in plenty of time for the game. How are you feeling?'

'Sick.'

'It's nerves,' said Dad. 'Damn. I forgot the cranberry sauce.'

'No one ever eats it anyway. I'm going back to bed.'

'No you don't. I'm going to make you a big bowl of porridge. Slow-release energy, just the job. Tracy? How do you make porridge?' He fished around in the cupboard.

'You need oats. Haven't got any. You should have said.' Mum licked the spoon clean of mincemeat and bent down to put the trays in the oven. 'Take these out in ten to fifteen minutes. If you let them burn, Christmas is off. Try and eat something, Charlotte. And Bob, stop fussing her.'

'I don't want anything to eat,' I said mutinously once Mum had gone. We compromised on tea and toast. Dad made me a huge pile and when I took a bite I found out I was starving. I sat and ate it all up in front of the television, engrossed in one of those daft family films they only ever put on at Christmas. It was only when Will came down an hour later and said, 'What's that smell?' I remembered the mince pies.

They were burnt to a cinder. There was nothing for it but to chuck them in the bin and start again.

'Don't tell your mum,' Dad said, looking them up in a recipe book.

'No more secrets you said,' I reminded him, but we did them between us, step by step. It was easy and this time we remembered to take them out. They were smashing, lovely golden pastry with mincemeat bubbling up at the sides, and they smelt delicious.

'I could get into this baking malarkey,' said Dad, pleased as punch. 'I could be like that chef who can't stop swearing. He took up cooking after he was injured at football.'

The door banged and Mum came in, carrying presents and some bottles of wine. 'Clients,' she said, placing them under the tree. 'Mmm, they look nice.' She picked up a mince pie and took a bite. 'Funny that, they're still warm.' Dad and I smiled innocently at each other.

Dad heated up some soup (being as he was now so good at cooking) and we sat round the table and ate it with warm crusty bread. Then it was time to get a move on. We clambered into the van, me definitely feeling sick now, and set off for the County Ground. When we got there the Cornish army was already queuing for the turnstiles to open, resplendent in black and yellow scarves and the odd Father Christmas hat.

'Make way!' said Dad, pushing me through the crowd, his hands protectively on my shoulders. 'Excuse me! Player here.' Mum rolled her eyes but lots of people clapped me on the back and said, 'Good luck' and 'You show 'em, love.'

Inside the changing room it was bedlam, with people pulling everything out of their bags and squealing, 'Oh no, I've forgotten my socks!' or 'Where's my lucky lippy?' or 'I've lost my scrunchie!' as if Johnny Wilkinson couldn't have kicked that legendary drop goal to win the World Cup if he hadn't had his special boxers on. (Perhaps he did. Who knows?)

I gave Becky a hug and changed up. Next to us Janine pulled her scrumcap down tight over her ears and Becky nudged me and grinned. As usual she was looking sensational. She had on fake tan and she'd done her hair in tiny French plaits all over her head and someone, her mum presumably, had threaded black and yellow ribbons through them.

'Bend over,' said Becky. She spritzed my roots with Chloe's volumising spray and mussed up my hair. 'There, that's better. Rock chick with a touch of grunge. We've got a lot of admirers out there today.'

'Is Dobbin coming?'

'You bet! Mind you, that could be because he wants to watch Cornwall slaughter Somerset after our game.' She pulled out an emery board and started filing her nails. 'Spider?'

'What?'

'I'm thinking of dumping Wayne.'

'You're not? I thought you really liked him.' And I'd only just got my head round her going out with him! All that anguish for nothing.

'I did. I do.' She pulled a face. 'But it's been nearly a month now and you know me, I get bored easily. Plenty more fish in the sea and all that.' She grinned. 'I'm saving myself for my leading man. When he hits his teens, I'm in there.'

'Don't you dare! You leave my little brother alone, I'm warning you!'

She laughed. 'It's you he likes anyway.'

'Who? Will?'

'No, you idiot, Wayne.'

'Get lost!'

'It's true. He always has done. It's just that I got in first.'

There was no time to go down this path because Phil came in for a pep talk. Soon after we stuck our gum-shields in (spoiling the rock-chick effect somewhat) and trooped out on to the field, me touching the picture of my predecessor, Harry Roberts, Olympic silver medallist, for luck, as we filed past. The crowd roared and clapped as we ran on and all my internal organs decided to do somersaults, made worse when the opposition came on and we discovered they were nearly all built on Marlene's scale.

'Shit!' said Janine. 'I only come up to their knees.'

I looked up towards the North Stand where a row of bees from my very own apiary sat – my lovely family decked out in black and yellow. Mum, Dad, Will, Gran and Granddad, who'd made sure he'd kept his walkabout wife under lock and key this morning, all in a line. They waved in unison and Gran fluttered the Cornish flag, white cross on a black background. I grinned and waved back. I was Queen Bee today.

By the time we'd spent ten minutes warming up, I was ready to enjoy the game. It was a perfect day for it, cold but clear with a light wind.

We were playing twelve aside across the field, the pitch marked out with cones, fifteen minutes each way. The linesmen took up their positions and the ref in his red shirt called for the toss. 'Heads,' said Janine who had the honour of being captain today, but it was tails. Somerset kicked off and we were away. Immediately I could distinguish Dad's voice from the rest of the crowd.

'Go on, Charlie, get it out!'

Shut up, Dad, I can do this on my own.

The opposition got off to a flying start and it was soon clear we were up against it. They were bigger and more powerful than us and had no trouble keeping the ball in their possession. Within minutes they'd driven over the line and grabbed the first try of the game and seconds later it was converted by their fly-half. Their fans went wild. They were good.

In the restart they secured the ball, passing it neatly down the field. We had to up our game.

'Make it yours, Charlie, make it yours!' Phil's voice filtered through from behind. I managed to intercept it and gave it to Crystal who cleared it into touch.

'Nice work!' yelled Phil but he spoke too soon. In the line-out one of their huge forwards soared into the air to gain repossession. Before she had time to clear it Becky appeared from nowhere to send her flying. What was she doing? Their player sat up, nursing a bloody nose. The crowd booed.

Becky was sent off to the sin-bin. The ref awarded a penalty against us and they seized the opportunity to drive the ball upfield and score another try. At half-time the score was 12–0 to Somerset.

Phil was beside himself with fury. 'What the hell were you playing at?' he bawled at Becky. 'Stay in position, the lot of you, and hold a defensive line. They're bigger than you so get that ball out to the wings. Some of you have left your brains at home!'

Becky was close to tears. We've blown it, I thought, we're outclassed. Then, as we ran back on the field, I glanced up at the North Stand and saw Will getting to his feet. He stood there, head erect, looking out over the pitch. Then Dad stood up next to him, turning to help Gran as she struggled to rise. Mum and Gramps stood up next, then everyone around them. What were they doing?

Then I heard it, quietly at first, like a hum, building up as more and more of the Cornish supporters got to their feet and joined in. And above them all, I don't know how, I could distinguish Will's voice, clear as a bell, leading them all in the first lines of the chorus that every Cornish rugby supporter knows by heart.

'And shall Trelawny live!
And shall Trelawny die?'

As if by magic, every Cornish voice in the stadium sang back the words,

'Here's twenty thousand Cornish men
Will know the reason why!'

As we took up our positions Will led the fans through all six verses of 'Trelawny', our rugby anthem, with literally thousands of Cornish supporters joining together for the chorus after each verse. By the time the game started again, we were so fired up I reckon we could have won the Six Nations. There was no way we were going to let that crowd down.

It was our ball. Janine tapped it back to me and we played a well-rehearsed set-piece. I passed it to Freya who cleared it to Janine. She belted down the wing, releasing the ball to Chloe when she was tackled by their scrum-half. Positioned in the centre, Chloe ran like she'd never run before in her life, to place the ball behind the line and bring us points on the board. The crowd roared.

Within seconds I'd converted it. 12–7. We were on our way.

Somerset mounted attack after attack but our defence had united. All our hours of tackling practice paid off. They might have been bigger than us but they didn't have our stamina and you could see they were running out of steam. Pocket-sized Janine, asthma firmly under control, tore down the pitch like a human dynamo, leaving them gasping behind. She was going to score a try.

Or she would have done if their ginormous full-back hadn't elbowed her as she flew past, sending her sprawling. Penalty to us! I placed it neatly between the posts. 12–10.

We'd clawed our way back.

'Spider!' I turned to look at Phil. He was pointing to his watch and holding up one finger. Shit! One minute to go.

Somerset kicked off and Crystal leapt to catch the ball. Almost immediately the whistle blasted. It was over; we'd run out of time. The visiting team whooped for joy and flung their arms round each other. I covered my face and sank to the ground.

The whistle blew again. And again. The victors stopped shrieking. I looked up. Everyone was staring at the ref who had his arm in the air.

'Penalty to Cornwall,' he said.

The crowd erupted.

'What?' I looked at Crystal for confirmation. She nodded, eyes shining.

'I was taken out in the air,' she said. 'It's up to you now.'

For a second panic set in. I couldn't do this on my own. I could hear Phil shouting instructions behind me but it was as if they had no meaning. I was going to mess up.

Then in my head I heard Dad's voice, cool and steady, as we kicked a ball round the back garden. 'Take your time, Charlie. Don't rush it.'

I looked up at the North Stand to locate my own hive of Roberts–Webb-Ellis bees among the swarm of black and yellow. Found them! Five white faces peered anxiously at me; no four, Mum's face was buried in her hands. But it was Dad's face I focused on and, as I watched, he cupped his hands round his mouth and yelled, 'Allow for the wind' and I nodded, and suddenly all my nerves left me and I felt deadly calm. I knew what I had to do.

I picked up the ball and placed it on the kicking tee. The ground fell silent.

I studied the post then took a deep breath. 'This one's for you, Dad,' I said aloud then I started my run-up. I struck the ball cleanly, taking into my calculations the light westerly wind, but as the ball soared into the sky, the wind appeared to drop.

As if in slow motion I watched as the ball curved in the air, a perfect arc, and swept down towards the goalposts. I'd pulled it too far to the left. The ball struck the upright first, then rebounded off the bar below before bouncing to the ground.

Did it fall in front of the posts?

Or behind?

I couldn't tell from this angle, but I heard the groan that came from the beehive in the North Stand.

My heart sank. Sorry, Dad. I screwed up.

The touch judges looked at each other then, as one man, they raised their flags and the ref blew for the match.

Cornwall went wild.

YEEEEEEEEES!

I'd done it.

We're all in the van and we're off to visit Gran. I've got something in my pocket to show her.

We pass the park. It's Sunday afternoon and everyone's out and about, enjoying the daffodils and the crocuses and the first warm rays of spring sunshine. Parents are pushing prams; dads are playing footie with their kids; joggers are weaving their way round the strolling couples. Mum and I exchange a rueful smile. We can't run on Sunday afternoons any more. We've got something else to do.

Dad pulls up at a crossing. 'Look, it's Phil and Bev!' Mum says in delight. Phil Brady, arm wrapped round his latest lady friend, is waiting to step down from the kerb. They smile and wave as they cross the road in front of us. We all wave back.

She got off with him in the end. She ran rings round him and finally scored in Bath. Good old Bev.

'Now she's teaching him a thing or two,' said Dad, and Mum chuckles. Will and I pull disgusted faces at each other.

I wonder if he knows she has her moustache zapped at Mum's salon every week?

I like Phil again now.

Soon we pull up at Granddad's. He's waiting for us at the gate holding a bunch of freshly picked daffs from his garden. He opens the back door of the van and climbs in beside Will and me.

'How did it go, Trace?'

'Brilliant!' Mum beams as she turns round to face Granddad. 'We didn't win, but boy, did we enjoy it.'

'That's what it's all about,' said Granddad, passing Will and me a chocolate éclair each out of his pocket. He's taken over the spoiling role since Gran's gone.

Mum's team played their friendly in February. They were hammered but Phil didn't seem too despondent. He organised a return match and worked on their shortcomings. The match was yesterday and they'd lost again but only just, this time. They've got another fixture booked before the end of the season.

It was Will's match that was amazing. That was the last game Gran went to see at the County Ground. The day before, the ground was frozen and Dad was paranoid it wouldn't pass inspection but there was a thaw overnight, thank goodness. They were solid teams, both of them, trained up to perfection, and I have to say, even though I'm biased, my kid brother's own lack of practice was more than compensated for by his natural talent. Cornwall won, 21–13, and Will scored two of the tries.

He's on his way to England, that boy.

So am I.

We drive on out of town, up towards the cemetery. Lots of daffodils here, and a few early blue irises and red and yellow and purple tulips too, bright splashes of colour amongst the grey granite graves.

We pass the wrought-iron gates and continue up the hill, bearing left to pull off the main road on to a sweeping drive, bordered by trees about to wake up after the long winter and break into leaf. Dad stops the van in front of a large white house, surrounded by long swathes of lawn. It looks like one of those country houses in films like *Pride and Prejudice*. Some of the residents are out on the grass in deckchairs, wrapped up warm and enjoying the sunshine. Most are elderly, but not all of them.

Gran's in a home now.

I was so angry when I found the letter.

Actually it was a brochure for a residential home. It had an application form inside.

'What's this?'

'It's for your gran,' said Mum, forgetting to tell me off

for being nosy. 'I was meaning to tell you. She's going to live there.'

'With Granddad? They're moving?'

'No. On her own. It's a nursing home. She needs special care now, twenty-four hours a day.'

I stared at her, aghast. 'You can't have her put away just because she's a nuisance!'

'It's not like that.' Mum looked upset. 'It's not a prison. It's very nice. Gran will be happy there.'

'No she won't. She'll hate it. Stuck in a home with loads of old people she doesn't know. She should be with us, we're her family!'

'Listen, love,' Mum's voice was gentle. 'Gran doesn't really know us any more. She doesn't know who *she* is half the time. She's become a danger to herself and she needs looking after full-time. It's not fair on Gramps.'

'We can look after her!'

Mum shook her head sadly. 'We can't, love.'

The funny thing is, Mum was right. Gran's settled in as if she's lived there all her life. Because as far as she's concerned, she has, in this weird twilight of a world she's living in now. We never really know who we're going to meet up with when we go to see her. Sometimes she thinks it's a school and she's the teacher; other times she's one of the pupils. Once she thought it was a hotel and she was a paying guest and Dad muttered, 'Dead right, five-star prices too,' but Mum shut him up with a look.

I think he's peeved because she never seems to recognise him. One day she thought he was a spy and told him to get out or she'd report him to the authorities. It's funny when you think he was always the centre of her world, but it's sad too. She seems to know Gramps, but even then, sometimes she calls him Doctor. But she's always pleased to see us.

'She's gone downhill very rapidly,' said Dr Keen, who still comes to visit her. 'But physically she's in good shape. She could go on like this for years.'

Poor Dad. He's so pleased to see how well looked after she is, but he can't help worrying about how much it's costing. And he's fed up at the moment because Mum's got him on a diet.

'If I can lose weight, so can you,' she said. She won't buy him any more cans from the supermarket either. It's doing him good actually; his beer belly's shrinking.

Today Gran is in the lounge, surrounded by her entourage. One of the things I was worried about was that she would be lonely, but she's such a chatterbox she's always got an audience of little white-haired old ladies round her. The gents seem to prefer the quiet life and avoid her. She's in full flood today, regaling them with some story or other, but she stops and beams when she spots us and abandons them all. I'm not sure she knows who we are but she's definitely glad we're here.

'Let's go and have a cup of tea in your room,' says Mum, taking her by the elbow. We crowd in and Mum makes the tea, handing it round with the biscuits she's brought. Will and I sit on Gran's bed and watch telly for a bit while she natters away to Mum and Dad. Snatches of her conversation drift in and out of my consciousness.

'It's nice to sit down, I haven't stopped all day. I've cleaned this place from top to bottom.'

'I'd better get a move on. You'll be wanting your dinner.'

'I'll tackle that washing in a minute. And I've got a pile of ironing to do.'

She's in busy-housewife-with-lots-of-children-to-look-after mode today. It all sounds sensible if you don't know her. There's a lull in the conversation and I try to look at my watch without Granddad noticing. I'm getting bored now. I wonder how long we're going to stay. Will nudges me.

'Show Gran your medal.'

I perk up. I love this bit. I take a tarnished silver case out of my pocket and press the little catch on the side.

'Look, Gran.'

She leans over obligingly to have a look and her face lights up when she spots the Olympic silver medal nestling in its red velvet bed. Her reaction is a joy to see and brings a smile to everyone's face even though we know what to expect.

'That's my father's medal,' she says, clear as a bell. 'It was his father's before him and it was passed on to my son. It'll be yours one day when you play for Cornwall.'

'I know, Gran. It is now.'

'You've played for Cornwall?' she asks, her voice reverent. 'Well I never.' She smiles at me fondly then the moment passes. Her eyes become vacant. After a while she turns to Mum.

'The meat's in the oven, I've just got the potatoes to do.'

She does it every time. It's as if the sight of the medal acts like those paddle things they use in hospital dramas to shock people back to life and just for a moment it jolts her back to Gran, my bossy, nosy, lovely gran with a finger in every pie and an absolute passion for the game of rugby. Then, like an electric current, it passes through, leaving her dislocated again.

Gramps blows his nose loudly. It's him I feel sorry for. He misses her.

Dad gave me the medal after I played against Somerset.

'It's yours,' he said. 'You've earned it.'

It was the proudest moment of my life.

'Now go on to play for England,' he said. 'Give your gran something to gloat about.'

Give him something to gloat about, he meant. Gran's gloating days were over.

'Like you should have done.'

He shrugged. 'It wasn't to be.'

'Dad?' I paused. I didn't know how to say this but I wanted him to know. 'I'm sorry Phil Brady's my coach.'

'Why?' Dad looked at me in surprise. 'He's good. He knows what he's doing.'

'No, you know . . . because he broke your leg . . .'

Because he shattered your dreams only to make mine come true, I really wanted to say.

Dad was silent for a while. I wish I'd kept my mouth shut.

'He didn't.'

'What?' Had I heard right?

Dad stood with his hands in his pockets, looking into the distance. I waited.

'It was my fault,' he said. He turned to face me and his face was sad. 'My own stupid fault. Nothing to do with him. I high-tackled him and smashed my leg as I came down. Served me right.'

'Oh, Dad.'

'Dirty play see, Charlie. That's the penalty you pay. Not much of a role model, am I?'

I flung my arms round him and he held me tight.

I love my dad.

When Will played for Cornwall in the New Year I thought I had to hand the medal over, but Dad said no, I had to hand it on to the next generation, it was a family tradition.

'Don't you mind, Will?'

He shook his head. He's never been one for collecting things. Although, there is a poster of him and Becky on his wall and I happen to know he's got a passport photo of her in the inside pocket of his schoolbag.

I'll kill her if she messes with him.

Not likely though. She's moved on to a Year 11 from her school since she dumped Dobbin.

Dobbin's coming with us to London next weekend. Now we're officially going out he gets invited on all the family outings by Mum who has been dying for me to have a boyfriend. It's embarrassing.

I don't feel as if I've got Becky's reject, honest. Far from it. I only went out with him in the first place because he convinced me that Becky was definitely second best.

'I wanted to ask you out for ages,' he explained. We'd got back on friendly terms and in the New Year he'd finally made it round for that help with his maths. I won't go into detail because some things should be kept private but let's just say one thing led to another and we soon abandoned Probability for predictability and now we're a couple.

'Why didn't you then?' I asked, nestled in his arms.

'I tried, but you're not the easiest person to pin down, Spider. First of all Phil Brady got in the way, then you slammed the phone down on me . . .'

Oops! I'd forgotten about that.

'. . . Then your dad told me to bugger off!'

Da-ad! I thought you were joking!

'. . . So you can hardly blame me for thinking you didn't want to know. I mean, you'd always made it clear you hated my guts.'

'That's not fair! You hated mine too!' I sat up indignantly.

'That's when we were kids. I've fancied you for ages.' I snuggled back happily. 'Then Becky asked me out and I thought, well, I've obviously got no chance with you, so I said yes.'

'So what would have happened if she hadn't dumped you?' I shot up again. 'You'd still be going out with her!'

'Don't be daft.' He pulled me down and kissed me. 'She only dumped me because she knew I liked you.'

Aah. Thanks, Becks.

I can't believe I used to hate Dobbin. He's the nicest bloke imaginable. And now his spots are gone and he makes me laugh and all the girls in my class think he's hot.

So next week we're all off to see England playing against Wales at Twickenham and Dobbin's coming too as a thank-you from Dad for rescuing Gran. Those two are bezzies now Dad's got over the shock of me actually being old enough to go out with someone and Dobbin's stopped worrying Dad will tell him to bugger off again.

In the evening we're going to the West End to see a musical. Dad nearly had a heart attack when he saw the prices. He PUT HIS FOOT DOWN and said we couldn't go and Will was gutted. But then Mum called Dad an old skinflint and said, never mind, we'd wait till we got to Leicester Square and take pot luck from the half-price tickets booth.

But I know, because he's let me into his secret, that the old skinflint's bought us all front-row tickets for *Billy Elliot*.

And the next day, Mum and I are abandoning the boys and are off to the high street to grab the latest spring fashions hot off the catwalk.

And actually, I can't wait.

A match, a musical, a mooch around the shops.

A-mazing.